Angela *nervou* *Christmas morning.*

She had no regrets. They'd driven out to the community pond and had a blast skating. They'd moved as one. She'd been amazed how right it had felt to be with David. He'd kissed her in the gazebo, and then again in the car before the drive back to her house. They'd steamed up the windows until they couldn't see out.

Not once had she asked herself what she was doing, because she knew. She was having fun. She was letting her attraction to David become more than a dream.

She was letting him in.

Available in December 2007 from Mills & Boon® Special Edition

A Texas Christmas
by Cathy Gillen Thacker

The Super Mum
by Karen Rose Smith

Sierra's Homecoming
by Linda Lael Miller

It Takes a Family
by Victoria Pade

Call Me Cowboy
by Judy Duarte

Under the Mistletoe
by Kristin Hardy

The Super Mum

KAREN
ROSE SMITH

MILLS & BOON
Pure reading pleasure

*First published in Great Britain 2007
by Harlequin Mills & Boon Limited,
Eton House, 18-24 Paradise Road, Richmond, Surrey TW9 1SR*

© Harlequin Books S.A. 2006

*Special thanks and acknowledgement are given to
Karen Rose Smith for her contribution to the* TALK OF THE
NEIGHBOURHOOD *mini-series.*

ISBN: 978 0 263 85666 8

23-1207

*Printed and bound in Spain
by Litografia Rosés S.A., Barcelona*

To Lisa Smith – Thank you for your thoughtfulness and support through a difficult time. May we always find that ray of sunshine and feel its warmth.

Chapter One

She was a fraud.

Everyone in the neighborhood thought Angela Schumacher was a Super mom, which might have been true a couple of years ago. But now, handling two jobs, caring for Olivia, Anthony and Michael more or less on her own, she was frazzled and on the edge.

She parked in her driveway and leaped out of her van, just staring at the scene in front of her. Evening light was fading fast. Her neighbor and babysitter, Zooey, stood just outside Angela's front door carrying Jack Lever's toddler. Zooey's hand was in a "stay" position to Olivia, Michael, and Jack's daughter, Emily, as she called to someone around the corner of the house.

Concerned that her normally unflappable, beautiful neighbor seemed hassled, Angela rushed forward. Although her blond hair was cut to a chic chin-length bob, and she usually felt good about herself when she looked in the mirror, next to Zooey she felt like a shrimp at five foot four. She'd never understood why it had taken Jack Lever so long to fall in love with his beautiful, willowy nanny. But he finally had, and everyone on Danbury Way had cheered. Now they were engaged to be married.

"Jack, be careful on that ladder," Zooey called around the corner of the house, her breath puffing white in the early December cold.

"What ladder?" Angela asked, astonished. What in the heck was going on here? Maybe a cat had climbed up onto the roof… "Why is Jack climbing a ladder?"

Shifting two-year-old Jack Jr. from one arm to the other, Zooey replied calmly, "It's Anthony."

The fact suddenly registered with Angela that Anthony wasn't standing in the doorway with the other kids. Her heart raced. Her mouth went dry. Panic clamped her chest. "What about Anthony? What's wrong? Why do you need a ladder? Is there a fire?"

Zooey gave her friend a hint of a smile. "No, no fire. Calm down. He's locked in his room. We can't get him to open the door. He and Olivia got into an argument. He took her rock collection, went into his room and locked everyone out."

Seven-year-old Olivia came rushing to Angela now, and so did Michael. "Mummy, I hate him," she cried, tears rolling down her cheeks. "He's got my rocks."

Olivia's rock collection was her most precious possession. That's obviously why Anthony had taken it. From the Super mom front, she was failing miserably with her oldest child. Anthony had been acting out in subtle ways for the past few months, ever since Jerome had missed his last two dates to see him.

Little Michael, whose fifth birthday seemed to give him permission to ask more questions than any other five-year-old in the world, gazed up at her with certainty.

"You can make him open the door. That's my room, too. He won't let me in."

"Jack just wanted to peek in the window to make sure he was okay," Zooey assured her.

At that moment Jack rounded the house and smiled at Angela. "He's as stubborn as any nine-year-old. He won't look at me or talk to me. He totally ignored me when I rapped on the window. But he's okay. He's sitting on his bed with his earphones on, playing with his GameBoy."

"I don't know what to do with him," Angela murmured. "I can't make up for what Jerome won't do."

After she shooed the other kids into the house, Zooey bounced Jack Jr. a bit. "Maybe it's time you look into the Big Brother program at the community center." She glanced at Jack for support.

He shrugged. "You'd get a positive, male influence that way. On the other hand, you could get married again…" As usual Jack's voice was full of mischief, and Angela knew he was just trying to make her smile. But right now, the idea of finding a husband ranked right up there with wanting to find a snake in her basement. She wasn't looking for one, didn't need one and would rather dismiss the whole scenario.

One thing she did know was that she had to take Anthony in hand. Up until now she'd been too lenient. She'd felt guilty because Jerome had left their Rosewood, New York, home without a backward glance. Disappointed he didn't understand what gems he had in his kids, sorry that they didn't feel his love, she'd overcompensated. That had to stop. Anthony had to understand reality, and she was going to explain it to him.

Turning to Zooey, she asked, "Can you stay for a few more minutes until I talk to Anthony?"

"No problem."

As Jack took Jack Jr. from Zooey's arms, he gave her a fast but resounding kiss. "Emily, are you coming with me?"

His daughter, the same age as Olivia, shook her head. "Olivia and I have stuff to talk about."

Jack raised his brows at Angela to ask what she thought.

She could imagine what stuff the two girls had to chatter about. But they were great friends, and Angela didn't mind Emily being around. "She can stay for supper if she'd like. I'm just going to make grilled cheese sandwiches and soup."

Jack whispered to Zooey, "Maybe we can convince Jack Jr. to go to bed early."

On a mission, Angela headed through the dining room to the kitchen, realizing how happy Zooey and Jack seemed. Planning their wedding for Valentine's Day, they were the picture of what a couple was supposed to be. She didn't believe she'd ever been that happy with Jerome.

They'd married because…

Because Angela had wanted a husband and a family. Her parents divorced when she was sixteen and her adopted sister, Megan, was fourteen. The break-up had hurt them both deeply. They'd turned to each other and were still best friends. Angela didn't know what she was going to do when Megan got married and moved out of the garage apartment after New Year's. Her sister had found love, too.

Maybe Angela had married Jerome because she'd wanted to believe in love…wanted to believe a man could stick better than her father had…wanted to believe in happy endings. But she'd learned the hard way that all men were alike. Well, maybe she was rethinking that a little because of the goings-on in the neighborhood. Megan and Greg seemed happy. Zooey and Jack couldn't take their eyes off each other. Her neighbor Carly and her husband Bo were opposites but seemed to fit together like two puzzle pieces. Neighbors Rebecca and Joe seemed content, too, and the buzz said they were going to get engaged any day.

Sometimes Angela felt as if she were operating in an alternate universe.

In the kitchen, Angela searched in the silverware drawer for a shish kebob skewer. Then she hurried upstairs, trying to figure out what to say to her oldest child.

At his door, she put the tip of the skewer in the small hole in the knob and popped the lock.

Anthony's room had been messier than ever the past two months—another aspect of his acting out. Although Michael was untidy in his little-boy-getting-older way— socks on the floor, toys not put back on the red-and-blue shelves—Anthony's messiness was different. It was deliberate. Candy bar wrappers lay strewn about. Half a banana sat rotting on his nightstand. There were clothes on the floor—his jeans and a shirt. His bedspread, patterned with soccer balls, baseballs and footballs lay sprawled over the footboard. She had a rule that the kids make their beds every day, and he'd been breaking it.

She had to take back control. She had to teach him he couldn't act however he wanted, that life wasn't always fair, that there were rules and boundaries.

When she approached the bed, he didn't even look up. He was sprawled there, one leg crossed over the other, headphones on, his fingers pressing buttons on his GameBoy. Determined to get his attention, she simply went to him and removed the earphones from his head.

"Hey!"

"I don't answer to *hey*. It's Mom. And when I come into the room, or when anybody comes into the room, you look at them."

His eyes went wide at her firm tone. Then he looked wary. He had Jerome's brown eyes. The same jaw, too. But he was as blond as she was. Even at nine he was already getting tall. He'd be six feet before long.

She motioned to the bed beside him. "Can I sit? We have to talk."

Again, that wary look and a half shrug.

"Things have to change around here. Especially your behavior."

A defensive frown shaped his mouth and, remaining silent, he folded his arms over his chest.

"I know you're upset because your dad canceled your last two outings. But you can't behave badly because of it. We can talk about it anytime you want."

"You're never here."

True she was at home a lot less than she used to be, but that couldn't be helped right now. "I'm here as much as I can be. I have to work to keep this house, to buy your clothes, to buy food. I'm working more now because with Aunt Megan leaving and getting married, we'll have more expenses. I'm looking for someone else to move in above the garage, but until I find that person, money's going to be tight."

His brows arched as if he'd never thought about all that.

"I don't want you to worry about it. We'll be okay. But that's why I took the part-time job at Felice's Nieces. I guess I should have explained all this to you before I did it. I forget that you're growing up."

When he lowered his eyes back to his GameBoy and didn't respond, she remembered Zooey's suggestion and plunged in. "There's a Big Brother program at the community center, and I'm going to look into getting you an older buddy who can do things with you."

"I want *Dad* to do things with me," he grumbled.

"I know you do. But I can't control what your dad does and neither can you. Instead of just being unhappy because he doesn't come around, we have to do something about it."

"I'm not going to hang out with some stranger!" Anthony exclaimed and rolled over on his side, turning his back to her. Angela sighed. Like everything else, this wasn't going to be easy. She could bake a great apple pie, but her life was falling apart and she had to do something about it.

Felice's Nieces, Rosewood's upscale 'tween and teen shop, was always loud, colorful and usually busy. Angela's full-time job as an office manager for a pediatric dentist was methodical and paperwork oriented. She actually enjoyed working here two nights a week, sometimes on Saturdays, and interacting with the kids. Besides that, she received a discount on her daughter's clothes.

As she separated ringspun denim jeans from sandblasted ones, she was aware of the plasma screen TV flickering with the latest DVD for the 'tween set. Surround sound blared from every direction.

Finished with the jeans, Angela moved toward a table laden with brightly colored sweaters. The kids picked at them and tossed them back down, and they constantly needed to be straightened. As she folded a lime one that Olivia might like for Christmas, the buzzer on the glass door sounded and she looked up.

Her heart beat faster as she examined the man who had just walked in. Tall, blond and broad-shouldered, he looked like every cheerleader's dream. Square-jawed, his face too rugged to be called handsome, he looked totally out of place amidst giggling girls, tall displays of jewelry and carousel racks filled with the latest styles. She couldn't quite gauge how old he was. Her age, maybe?

Reluctantly she returned her attention to the sweaters on the table, taking another peek at him as he went to the cashier's desk and spoke to the manager. Those shoulders filled out the hunter-green sweater to perfection. She could only imagine the muscles there. His gray stone-washed jeans fit his backside even better. The cross trainers he wore were expensive, and she wondered if he'd come in to buy somebody a Christmas present.

Stop it, she scolded herself. *As if you'd consider getting involved with anyone right now, let alone a hunk who'd be scared to death of three kids and a mortgage payment the size of the Eastern Seaboard.*

Angela was stacking sweaters into a neat pile when a deep male voice made her jump.

"Are you Angela Schumacher?"

Spinning around, clutching a sweater to her chest, she

looked up into the fascinating hazel eyes of the blond man who'd walked in a few minutes before.

Flustered, she had trouble finding her voice. Finally she managed to say, "I'm Angela."

He extended his hand. "I'm David Moore. I've been selected to be Anthony's Big Brother."

"I see," she replied inanely, not knowing what else to say. His hand was still extended and she slipped hers into it, immediately aware of the heat shooting up her arm, the increased rate of her pulse, the giddy feeling *she* hadn't experienced since she was a teenager.

Composing herself, she pulled her hand away. "The community center said you'd give me a call before you stopped by the house."

"When I called your house and explained who I was, your sitter told me you were working here tonight. Zooey, her name is."

"Oh, Zooey's my neighbor. She's watching the kids for me while my sister's on a business trip and…" She trailed off feeling foolish. "It's complicated."

"Life usually is."

His smile curled her toes. What was wrong with her? Her ex-husband had taught her many lessons and she'd remembered them all. She wanted nothing to do with another relationship.

A little voice she didn't recognize whispered, *Who's talking about a relationship? What about a torrid affair?*

Feeling herself flush, Angela asked, "Do you live near here?" She still didn't understand why he had just dropped in.

"No. But my store's across the plaza—Moore's Sporting Goods."

She hadn't made the connection. "That's you?"

"That's me. I coach high-school football on the side. That's how I got involved with the mentoring program."

His hazel eyes turned a bit greener, and Angela wondered how old he really was, how he'd come to own a sporting goods store and why he coached on the side. Too many questions. She didn't care, did she? Well, she cared where Anthony's well-being was at stake. She really didn't know anything about this man…

As if he'd read her thoughts, he took a folded sheet of paper out of his back pocket, unfolded it and handed it to her. "Here are my stats with basic information and the names of parents of kids I've mentored. If you don't like what you see there or you don't get the information you want to hear from my references, you can choose another mentor. I know these days parents need to check out anyone who will be spending time with their kids."

"Do you have children?"

"No."

That's all he said, but he wasn't wearing a wedding ring. The absence of one didn't mean anything, and besides, she shouldn't even be looking.

"I thought I could spend some time with Anthony on Saturday."

She'd have two days to check out his references. That should be enough time. "I work here in the morning, but afternoon would be okay. I have to tell you, though, my son doesn't like the idea of a mentor *or* a Big Brother."

"He might change his mind once we actually do some fun stuff. We'll go easy and take it a little at a time."

Her gaze fell to his lips and she felt that giddiness again. A little at a time. Is that the way he handled women, too? Shoot. Something must have triggered hormones she didn't even know she had.

Someone nudged Angela's elbow. "Ms. Schumacher? Does this go together?"

Angela looked down at Denise, a twelve-year-old who often came into the store without her mom.

"You're busy," David Moore remarked. "I don't want to take up your time. "I'll see you Saturday afternoon."

"Saturday afternoon," she repeated, reminding herself she needed help with Anthony, not a hot affair.

Then she laughed inwardly. Who could possibly have a hot affair with three kids around?

Angela shook her gloved hands, trying to bring some warmth back into them. Snow had fallen last night into this morning. Even though it was early December, the four inches that had fluttered down like fairy dust had collected and stayed. She knew she should probably wait to tack up the string of lights around her front door, but she had time right now, and that was something she didn't often have. The sky was gray, as if snow could fall again at any minute, and the temperature hovered at freezing.

Angela concentrated on climbing the small ladder carefully and attaching nail-on clips that would hold icicle lights around the perimeter of the porch roof. Her two-story Colonial was gray-and-white brick. The breezeway attaching the garage to the house sported white siding with gray shutters. She loved the house and it suited her needs perfectly. After Jerome left, she'd used her settlement to turn the space above the garage into an apartment for Megan. The arrangement had worked well for both of them. But at the end of the month Megan would be moving out, and Angela would have to cover the entire mortgage herself, as well as the utilities, until she found a renter. The problem was she couldn't let just anyone move in. It had to be someone she could trust around her kids.

The purr of a vehicle's engine along Danbury Way slowed. Angela didn't pay much attention. There were nine houses in the cul-de-sac; somebody was always coming and going. However, the vehicle pulled into *her* driveway. When she heard the slam of the door, she finished hammering in a clip then turned to look.

She almost lost her balance. David Moore was walking toward her, and she realized she was surprised. She'd half expected him not to show up, even though his references had said he was reliable. According to them, he'd kept all his appointments with their kids. But in Angela's experience men usually bowed out of important events, didn't stick around *or* keep vows.

"That doesn't look too steady," David noticed, as he motioned to the rickety ladder.

"I only have a few more clips left, then I'll be finished."

"It might be easier for someone taller to do it. I don't have to reach as high. Come on, let me help you down."

He was so tall, maybe six-two. From up here she could see his hair was a mixture of brown and blond. He seemed to have a tan that could be year-round, and she guessed the sun streaked his hair, whether he was skiing or swimming. There was no doubt he was athletic.

When he offered her his arm, covered by the red down

jacket, she took hold of it, noticing how strong it was. At five-four and 105 pounds, she felt fragile as she stepped down and stood before him.

"I didn't get a call from the community center saying you didn't want me to come. You checked the references?"

"Yes. Everybody gave you glowing recommendations."

"I enjoy being with the kids and I hope they enjoy being with me. That's what matters."

Whatever David Moore had been or was now, his ego didn't seem to be as big as her house.

David took the hammer from her hand and went up the first step of the ladder. "Clips?" he asked.

Taking a few from her pocket, she handed them to him. In less time than it would have taken her, he had the lights fastened along the edge of the porch roof.

Facing her again, he asked, "Is Anthony around?"

"He's up in his room, sulking. I told him you might come by. He wants no part of a Big Brother. So he says."

Whenever she looked into David Moore's eyes, she felt…stunned in some way. From the stat sheet he'd given her, she had seen he was twenty-eight, three years younger than she was. She'd never entertained the idea of being attracted to a younger man. Even before Jerome, she'd seemed to be attracted to men older than she was. But there was something about David that was so…breath catching.

"Since he's not in favor of this idea, maybe we should go at it sideways," David suggested.

"Sideways?"

"Kids are taking advantage of the first snow and tubing down the hill near the reservoir. I saw them when I drove in."

She understood what he meant. "Anthony has a sled."

"The social worker who works with the community center said Anthony has a sister who's seven and a brother who's five. Do you think they'd like to go, too? If we made this a group outing, maybe Anthony would get used to me."

"You want me to go along?"

"Wouldn't you feel better about me spending time with Anthony if you were around?"

This man was perceptive. "Actually, I would. I didn't like the idea of you just taking him away somewhere. Not yet, anyway."

"Then sledding it is. Hopefully I can ease into a friendship without a lot of pressure on him to accept me."

"I could make cocoa to take along, and I baked a batch of cookies when I got home. We can take those, too." She didn't have the reputation of being Super mom for nothing.

"A woman who actually bakes!" he commented with a grin. "You're a lost breed."

She laughed, a bit self-consciously. "I like to cook and experiment with recipes. Especially desserts."

His gaze slid over her fitted green wool jacket and black leggings. "You mustn't eat them."

She blushed, feeling foolish. "I eat my share. I'm just so busy running from one job to another and taking care of the kids, I must burn it off." She began to fold the ladder.

"I can get that. Does it go in the garage?"

She nodded. "You can come into the house and go

through the breezeway off the kitchen. I'll round up the kids and tell them to get ready."

Olivia and Michael, who were watching TV, looked interested when Angela introduced David. After she explained they were going to go sledding, they gave a "whoop" and ran to their rooms to dress warmly.

Standing in the foyer, she called up the stairs. "Anthony. Come here a minute, will you? Mr. Moore is here."

Anthony came to the top of the stairs and gazed down at her and David.

"Come on down," she said, hoping he wouldn't be rude. She'd been firmer with him since the day he'd locked himself in his room, and he wasn't happy about it.

When he reached the bottom step, David extended his hand to him. "Hi, I'm David Moore."

"I don't need anyone to take me to the movies or treat me like a kid," Anthony said defensively.

"I guess you don't. And you're old enough to know what you want to do. But I thought all of us could try out this snow. I put tubes in the back of my SUV and I've got a toboggan, too. Or, you can take your own sled. I thought we'd all go."

Anthony looked at his mother. "You're going to go sledding?"

"I just might. I'm not over the hill yet." She didn't know why she'd said that.

"You could break something," Anthony mumbled.

David laughed. "Maybe you and I will just have to make sure she doesn't."

It was obvious that Anthony was fighting a battle within. He didn't want to go along with David, but he liked the idea of sledding. Or tubing. Or tobogganing. "Olivia and Michael are going, too?"

"Sure. We can all use the fresh air," Angela remarked, as if it weren't a big thing to go on a family outing. They rarely did that anymore. Since Jerome left, outings emphasized his absence. Not that he'd been great at family activities. When they were married, he'd worked late and had always done his own thing on weekends.

It had taken Angela too long to catch on to what her husband's own thing was. But she *had* caught on and had confronted him with a woman's bracelet she'd found in the pocket of his suit jacket. Then her next-door neighbor, Judith Martin, had told her she'd seen Jerome and a redhead having a late dinner at Entrée, a trendy restaurant in town that another one of her neighbor's owned. Jerome had insisted it was a business dinner, but she'd figured otherwise. He'd taken the woman to that particular restaurant so it would get back to her. He'd wanted out. She'd suggested counseling, but he'd just laughed, hurting her big-time when he admitted he wasn't meant to be monogamous—it simply wasn't in his nature.

When he'd left that evening, he'd seemed happy about changing his life. She'd cried herself to sleep every night for about two weeks. Then, after a heart-to-heart with her sister, she'd known she was better off without him. He'd chipped off a piece of her heart, though, and although it had been three years, the wound hadn't completely healed.

"Do you know where my boots are?" Anthony asked, being practical.

"I think they're in the basement. While you change, I'll get them. Tell Olivia and Michael to put sweaters on under their parkas."

Anthony made a face, then ran up the stairs.

By the time Angela found the kids' boots and her own, David was back in the kitchen, shedding his coat. "If I help you, we'll get out of here sooner—before Anthony changes his mind."

The truth was, she wasn't used to having a man in her kitchen anymore. Since her divorce, she'd become independent in every sense of the word and in every part of her life.

"What would you like to help with?" she asked cautiously.

"I make great hot chocolate, with milk and an instant mix. Is that what you were planning on doing?"

"Actually, it was." When she smiled at him, she felt that heart-twirling sensation again.

Trying to chill, trying to ignore tingles running through the body she no longer knew, she motioned to a lower cupboard. "Saucepan is down there. Hot chocolate mix is in that jar." She pointed to a mason jar on the counter next to a row of ceramic canisters.

When she reached above her to get a thermos from the upper cupboard, she had to stand on her tiptoes. But the thermos was pushed back on the shelf, just out of her reach.

"Here, let me." He was behind her then, and she could feel the strength of him...the heat of him...smell his limy scent as he reached above her.

"I'm too short," she mumbled. "Megan can reach up there. She must have put it there."

"Megan?"

"She's my sister. She lives in the apartment above the garage. She usually helps me with the kids, but she's away on business now. My neighbor across the street has been helping out."

When he lowered the thermos, he set it on the counter, and they were very close, his elbow brushing hers.

She had to get a grip. She was going to be in the presence of this man the whole afternoon, and she couldn't act like an idiot.

"I noticed Anthony's name is different from yours."

Making the decision to take back her maiden name hadn't been easy, because she hadn't wanted to affect the kids, who had of course kept Jerome's surname of Buffington. But she'd needed that piece of paper reiterating her independence in that way, too. "I took back my maiden name after my divorce."

"Bitter divorce?"

"It could have been more amicable, I guess, but we tried to put the kids first."

"But now your ex-husband isn't putting the kids first?"

This man was a stranger, yet he deserved to understand the situation so he could relate to Anthony. "Jerome isn't the most dependable man on earth. He's missed his last two dates with the kids. Anthony, especially, has reacted to that. I'm afraid he thinks his dad doesn't love him. I've called Jerome and left messages but he doesn't call back. The truth is—I think he sees my number on his caller ID and ignores us."

"And this is why you called the community center?"

"We had an incident earlier in the week. Anthony locked himself in his room. A neighbor suggested the Big Brother program. I'm willing to try anything. I don't want him to turn into a defiant teenager."

Nodding solemnly, David moved a few steps away to retrieve the packets of hot chocolate.

Angela felt as if she could breathe again.

Now that he knew something about her, she wanted to know more than statistics about him. "Is your family around here?"

After a moment's hesitation, he explained, "My dad lives about an hour north and I have a sister another half hour from there. I don't see them as much as I should."

"I know what you mean. Life gets too busy. Since Megan got engaged, I don't see as much of her as I used to."

"That happened recently?"

"July. She and Greg are getting married on New Year's Eve." Angela sighed. "I'm going to miss her when she moves out."

"Is she moving far away?"

"No, they'll be staying in Rosewood. But…it won't be the same. She was a great support after my divorce. She's my best friend."

He was listening to her, looking at her as if he understood every word she said. When had a man ever listened to her? *Really* listened?

He's younger than you, a scolding voice in her head warned her. *And you have three kids,* it added, as if the age difference weren't enough.

However, David was looking at her as if they were the only two people on earth. Her fingers practically itched to sift through his brown blond hair that fell rakishly over his brow. The scent of his aftershave drew her closer, as did the gold sparks in his hazel eyes.

He lifted his arm…

Was he going to touch her cheek? Was he going to bend his head and kiss her?

The zip of sexual attraction bounced between them as she waited breathlessly.

Chapter Two

David knew he had to deep-six any desire he felt for this woman. Escaping from whatever had come over him, he straightened and took a healthy step away from her. "I'd better get the milk going."

She blinked those very blue eyes at him. What was it about Angela Schumacher that got to him?

"Sure." A look of self-protective pride spread over her face, mixing with another emotion. Disappointment maybe?

They weren't going to talk about what almost happened. That would make it more real. At this point, he could turn off his attraction to her and set himself on the right course. He was here because of her son.

End of story.

She busied herself wrapping cookies in tin foil. "Sledding will be a real treat for the kids today. Last year we only went twice. Did you go often as a kid?"

The questions about his background shouldn't have thrown him, but they did. He didn't know how much he wanted to reveal. It wasn't as if he had anything to hide—his life was an open book, if anybody wanted to look. But his life *hadn't* ended up where he thought it would, and there had been disappointments along the way for him, as well as his family.

"We lived on a farm, so there were a lot of places to go sledding."

"What kind of farm?" She looked genuinely interested.

"A dairy farm. Dad still keeps it all running, but I don't know how much longer he can do that."

"What about your mom?"

"She died when I was in my teens—of ovarian cancer."

"I'm so sorry. Losing a parent is rough. My parents were divorced, and I didn't see my dad much after that. It's not nearly the same thing, but it's why I know how Anthony feels," she said.

"We'll see if we can't do something about that, starting today."

The smile she gave him tightened his gut and made other physical reactions start happening, too. He wondered if she knew what a powerful punch she packed as a woman.

He was going to stay out of striking range.

By the time he and Angela finished in the kitchen, the kids were dressed and ready to go. Anthony wasn't coming anywhere near David, but that was okay.

Angela had taken a few minutes to slip into ski pants and a jacket. The outfit was a brilliant turquoise with a yellow stripe. She was petite but not demure. Feminine, yet not passive. He thought of the fiancée who'd left him because his career had been ruined…because she'd wanted some of the fame his dad had dreamed of for him. Jessica's leaving while he'd worked in rehab to regain use of his leg had seemed like a crushing defeat. Fate double dealing him. At twenty-eight, he still couldn't figure out women, and for the past couple of years had stopped trying. He dated, but never seriously. Sometimes he felt as if he were out of step with the rest of the men of his generation who hopped from one woman's bed to another, as if sex and relationships were some kind of game. Maybe it was his upbringing, but he'd never felt like that.

A half hour later, as David unloaded his toboggan from the rack on his SUV, he saw Angela lifting a saucer from her van. Michael grabbed it and, struggling with it, took off through the cluster of kids and adults at the top of the hill.

"Michael, wait," Angela called after him.

David hollered over to her, "I'll watch out for him. Take your time." He started off toward Michael.

Soon he was aware of Anthony following, a good ten feet behind him. This Big Brother thing was going to be a hard sell. But if he didn't push, the nine-year-old might come around. Most kids did because they missed the male figure in their life who wasn't there anymore… because they felt as if a piece of their life was missing.

The next hour seemed to fly by in a mixture of runs down the hill, trudges back up, laughter and adrenaline rushes—mostly because of getting too close to Angela, not the speed of sledding down the hill.

Anthony just sort of buzzed around at a distance,

giving David curious looks now and then, acting sullen and withdrawn otherwise. He'd met up with a friend, and at one point the two boys had joined David on the toboggan. Afterward, Anthony had gone his way again. As Angela kept a close eye on everyone, David noticed she oversaw the outing but didn't sled herself. Did she feel she couldn't have fun when the kids were around?

Although she was holding a cup of hot chocolate and breathing in the warmth, her nose and cheeks were red. They'd have to leave soon.

In spite of an inner voice telling him to stay removed, David approached her. "How about taking a run down the hill with me?"

"I don't think so," she answered politely.

"Are you afraid I'll dump you in the snow?"

She gave him a genuine smile. "Maybe. I'm not a speed junkie."

"You don't like roller coasters?"

"I avoid them at all costs. I turn an ugly shade of green."

"I doubt that. Come on. You need to show your kids you can join in the fun."

"I do?" She looked a bit defensive.

"Sure. I think one of the reasons kids keep a distance from their parents is because they think their parents were never kids. Or have forgotten what it was like to be a kid."

As she gazed out over the snow-covered vista and the pines beyond, she seemed to think that over. Her focus went to Olivia, who was tubing down the hill with a friend. Then she concentrated on Michael, who was in his own world, spinning his saucer on a snow patch.

Anthony had taken his sled and was doing belly flops down the hill.

A tall man had arrived a few minutes ago with his daughter, and Angela had spoken to him for a while. David had definitely noticed. That same man was standing by a picnic table, watching his daughter, who was sledding with Olivia.

"Hey, Jack," Angela called to him. "Can you keep an eye on my kids for a few minutes?"

"No problem," he called back.

She turned back to David, "All right," she agreed. "*One* run."

"You have to smile, so they think you're having fun even when you're not."

She laughed, and he liked the sound of it. He liked her.

A few minutes later he was positioning the toboggan. "It'll be easier if I hop on first. Then you slide back between my legs."

Her eyes grew a bit bluer and wider, and for a moment she looked as if she wanted to run. Maybe he'd been wrong about a mutual attraction. Maybe it had been wishful thinking.

"This will be over quicker than you can say your name." He hopped on before she could change her mind, then motioned in front of him.

After brief moments of hesitation, she sat at the foot of the toboggan, then levered herself backward until she was between his legs, closer to his chest.

He realized he was going to have to put his arms around her to guide the toboggan, unless she wanted to handle steering. "If you want me to guide the sled, I'm going to have to put my arms around you and take hold of the lead."

"Fine," came her small low voice.

This had been such a *bad* idea. His knees were lodged against her hips. After he slid forward, his arms went around her and he felt her tense. But then she handed him the rope.

"Stay loose," he warned her, his chin practically touching her shoulder. "If we do capsize, it'll make the tumble easier."

"Do I *really* want to do this?" she muttered, looking toward heaven.

His arms were under hers now. In spite of the cold he felt the warmth from her body, the heat of whatever sexual attraction was zipping between them. It *wasn't* one-sided.

She wore a pull-on knit cap, and it almost touched his nose as he used his leg to push them off. "Hold on," he suggested as they tilted over the crest of the hill and began their descent.

She did hold on. Her hands clasped his arms, and the rush of wind, the bite of cold rising from the snow, the accelerated speed as they picked up velocity, weren't as thrilling as having this woman in his arms. As they flew down the hill, she lay into his chest. He leaned forward to protect her. The ride was exhilarating. Her perfume mingling with the pine and winter was intoxicating. The rush that went through him surpassed anything he'd ever felt on the football field. That was most surprising of all. He'd thought he'd lost that adrenaline lift forever. But here it was today, because of Angela Schumacher.

The ride was over as quickly as it had begun. One

moment the toboggan was speeding, the downhill slope propelling it. The next they were coasting to a stop.

Neither of them spoke or moved, although other sleds and tubes careered down the hill around them. Riders jumped off, grabbed their leads and marched up the hill again for another run.

But David and Angela just sat there.

"That was something," he said just to get her to talk.

When she glanced over her shoulder, their faces were very close. "It was indescribable."

Her lips were so prettily curved, her chin as petite and delicate as the rest of her. He wanted to kiss her more than he wanted to take another ride like that. But if he did, he'd ruin his chance to get to know Anthony. He'd ruin their chances of maybe becoming friends. He'd ruin the path he'd set for himself to make success a priority, his store and working with kids all the purpose in life he needed.

He inched back away from her. "I'm glad you liked it."

When she saw he was extricating himself, she slid forward and then climbed to her feet. Slapping her hands together to warm them, she grimaced. "I think it's time to go. The kids have got to be as cold as I am."

He wasn't cold at all because of the fire that had started burning inside of him—a fire he knew could only lead to trouble. "Maybe we could round them up and have more of that hot chocolate. Anthony hasn't even looked me directly in the eyes yet today, and I'd like to accomplish at least that much."

"Hot chocolate it is. I think there are a few cookies left, too."

They began trudging up the hill. The snow was

wearing an icy sheen from the movement of the sleds on top of it. Near the top, one of Angela's booted feet slipped.

Before she could topple sideways, David wrapped an arm around her. They were body to body again, and he wondered if he should have just let her fall.

But he couldn't have done that.

As soon as she regained her balance, she pushed away. "Thanks," she mumbled, negotiating the rest of the climb herself.

David was beginning to see that Angela Schumacher was a modern day, independent woman.

Maybe.

Jessica had taught him that actions weren't always a good indicator of what was going on inside a woman's head. After the accident that had killed one of his friends and ruined his career, she could have earned an Academy Award for her smiling visits of support, the cards she sent him in rehab, the telephone calls that had assured him he'd be on top of the world again in no time.

The day after the accident, everyone had known his NFL dreams were dust. Including Jessica. Maybe she really hadn't known how she'd felt. Maybe she'd been trying out a role to see how it fit. Maybe she hadn't felt any love at all, but had simply wanted to ride his jersey into a life of fame, fortune, big houses and luxurious cars. She'd walked away because she'd signed up for a fiancé different from the one she'd gotten.

Loyalty and promises kept were rare commodities these days.

Angela was shaking when she reached the top of the hill. Her trembling had nothing to do with the cold and everything to do with David Moore. Teenage crushes were long ago and far away and had no right to reach out and grab her now. Just because his eyes seemed to swallow her up. Just because his smile made her toes curl. Just because he listened as if she really had something to say. None of that could excuse this reaction.

Olivia came running over to her.

With a nonchalance she wished *she* could feel, David offered, "I'll round up Michael and Anthony and stow their gear."

"I'll warm up the van and get out the snacks."

As Olivia dragged her tube behind her, they walked toward the van in the parking lot. "Do we have to go home?"

"Sure do. You're going to turn into an icicle otherwise."

When Angela pressed the remote to open the doors, Olivia asked, "How did it feel going down the hill with Coach Moore?"

What should a mother say to that? "It was over so fast I hardly remember it."

Liar, an inner voice accused.

"He's a real hottie, isn't he?"

Angela just stared at her daughter. She was only seven, for goodness sakes. "*Where* do you pick up this language?"

"I watch TV," her daughter said impishly, then added, "I hear the middle-school girls talking on the bus. Everybody does. I don't live in a bubble, Mom."

Whatever happened to seven-year-olds playing with baby dolls, putting puzzles together or skipping rope with friends? Even Olivia wanted an MP3 player for Christmas, and Angela had no doubts she probably knew how to use one.

Still with that grin, her daughter added, "I think you like him."

Oh, terrific! Apparently her reactions to the man were obvious even to Olivia.

"Coach Moore is going to spend some time with Anthony, I hope. That's it."

"You don't want to go out with him?" Olivia asked with her eyes narrowing.

"Of course not. When would I even have time?" She dropped her arm around Olivia's shoulders. "I've got a life daughter, dear. I've got you and Anthony and Michael. What more do I need?"

"You still miss Daddy, don't you?"

As always, when her kids asked a question like that, Angela paid complete attention. Dropping down to Olivia's eye level she admitted, "I miss what we once had. I miss another adult in the house to talk to...someone I'm connected with in a special way. But I can't control what your dad does. I wish he'd visit with all of you more, but he's trying to get a new business up and running, and that keeps him busy." At least that was the excuse Jerome was giving. It was also his excuse for not sending timely child support payments.

"I miss Daddy, but I don't miss you and him arguing about him never being there."

Kids saw and heard *everything* and she had to remind herself of that every day. "Things are just different now. We're a different kind of family. And that's okay."

"So..." Olivia drawled. "Don't you want to go to the movies or something with Coach Moore?"

"No," Angela returned, straightening. "That's not on the

agenda. As I said, he's going to be Anthony's friend. Then maybe your brother won't be so miserable all the time."

"Yeah. Then maybe he'll stay out of my room."

Ten minutes later they were inside the van, drinking hot chocolate and munching on chocolate chip cookies. David had encouraged Olivia to take the front seat beside her mom while he sat in back of Angela and Anthony sat beside him. Of his own accord, Michael had crawled into the van's third seat. They'd left the door open a bit on Anthony's side.

"Your mom makes great cookies," David commented.

"Some moms don't bake at all," Olivia remarked over her shoulder, sounding shocked, as if that was inconceivable.

Suddenly one of Anthony's friends was standing at the van door.

"Hi, Simon," Angela greeted him. Simon was in Anthony's class and also had played Little League with him.

Simon pointed to David. "My dad says he played for the NFL."

Anthony cut a sideways glance to David. "You didn't tell me that. Is that true?"

Angela was all ears herself.

"I was *drafted* by the NFL and I went to training camp, but I never got a chance to play. I was in a car accident that messed up my leg."

"That was rotten luck," Simon stated emphatically. "My dad says you're a great coach, now, though. The Raiders won almost all their games."

"Your dad must be a football fan."

"He's always in front of the TV watching sports of

some kind. Mom doesn't like it. That's why she said we're gonna cut down a Christmas tree tomorrow, and he has to go along."

"That'd be neat to cut down a Christmas tree," Anthony said wistfully.

Angela saw David studying her son. Then he said, "I'm great with a saw. If you and your mom want to pick out a tree, I could cut it down for you."

"Can we do that, Mom?" Anthony asked, excited.

Angela loved seeing that sparkle in her son's eyes. She'd missed it the past few weeks. If cutting down a Christmas tree would help put a smile on his face, she'd freeze off her toes and fingers again tomorrow. She was also willing to try to put her reactions to David into deep freeze, too. "If Coach Moore's willing to saw it for us, I guess we can."

"That's a plan, then," David stated. "Why don't I meet you at the Christmas tree farm around two?"

"Two will be fine." Angela told herself she was just looking forward to the outing because it was something Anthony wanted to do for a change. It didn't have anything to do with the fact that David would be along.

After Simon had taken off for his family's car, David opened the door on her side of the van. "I'd better be shoving off."

"Wait," she called, before she thought better of it.

Already out of the van, David closed the door and stood before her window.

When she pressed the button, it rolled down a bit. "Thank you," she said softly, meaning it. "Are you sure you want to go tomorrow?"

"I'm sure. It's been a long time since I've cut down a Christmas tree. I'll see you at two."

With a wave, he headed off toward his SUV, and Angela couldn't help staring after him. He was three years younger than she was, a bachelor and way too intriguing. Reluctantly, and with a sigh, she came back to reality. She was a single mom with responsibilities and no spare time. This outing tomorrow was for her children's sake, and she wouldn't forget that.

After Anthony closed his side of the van, she switched on the ignition. "Buckle up."

As the kids fastened their seat belts, she did the same, all the while remembering the feel of David's body around hers as they'd sped down the hill. For those few moments, she'd felt young and free and alive again.

With another sigh she backed out of the parking place and started for home.

As Olivia, Michael and Anthony ran from tree to tree, squabbling about which one would be perfect in their living room, David asked Angela, "Do they ever agree?"

She laughed. "Once in a great while. I'm just so glad to see Anthony is a part of this today. He's actually excited about something. He's been moping around for so long, I was afraid he'd forgotten how to have fun."

To his surprise, David was having fun, too. He usually related to kids one-on-one, not in a family setting. This was different. But there was no other way to reach out to Anthony and have him reach back.

As spokesman, Anthony ran over to them and pointed to a Douglas fir. "That's the one we want."

Michael complained, "I like the one over there."

"It's not as tall," Olivia berated him. "We want a *tall* tree."

Out of the blue, as if he'd been thinking about it all day, Anthony asked David, "I know you don't play in the NFL, but do you know guys who do? I mean, you went to their training camp and all."

"I've kept in contact with a few. Do you know Duke Smith of the Redskins?"

"Wow! Duke Smith! Yeah, I watch him on TV." Anthony looked at the tree and then back at David. "Maybe you'd like to help us put up the tree. Whaddya think, Mom? Can he?"

"*And* he can stay for supper," Olivia piped up.

Angela looked flabbergasted by her daughter's invitation.

If he helped with the tree, David knew more questions about football were going to come up. He also knew something else might come up that he should probably tell Angela about. It was the incident that had started him mentoring in the first place. Yet all of it was personal, and he and Angela weren't on that level yet.

When he was silent, Angela recovered her composure and asked, "Do you have other plans? You probably cherish your free time on weekends."

"I do. But I haven't helped put up a Christmas tree in years. Are you sure you want me there?" he asked Anthony, looking straight at him.

The boy met his eyes this time. "Yeah. Last year Mom tried to do it herself and the whole thing fell over the next day. It was a mess."

When Angela laughed self-consciously, David could have kissed her. She was so cute when she blushed. "Your son is a practical kid."

"He doesn't want more of his favorite ornaments to break. I can't say I blame him."

"At least they picked a straight tree." He grinned, as he took his saw from the sled they'd brought along to transport the tree.

After David cut down the fir and arranged it on the sled, Anthony asked if he could pull it, and Michael insisted on helping. David motioned down the trail to the barn where the proprietor of the farm was bagging the trees so they were easier to take home. All the kids started down the hill, cooperating for a change.

"That won't last long," Angela said with a smile.

David knew Olivia's invitation had taken Angela aback. "I don't have to stay for supper. I know you weren't prepared for that."

For a few moments, she looked over the rows and rows of fir trees, as if debating with herself. Then she said, "All the kids want you there. I think they're starved for a father figure. The question is, do you want to be that? Mentoring Anthony is one thing. Having two other kids pile on is another."

"You've got great kids. I'm a novelty right now. Hopefully Anthony and I can form a friendship that will help him. But if your other two kids want to be part of that, I don't mind. I intend to give Anthony alone time, though, because I think that's what he needs."

"You're right about that. He and Jerome never spent a lot of time together, but whenever he could, Anthony tagged along with his dad."

"We could just stop for a pizza on the way home," David suggested, not wanting to put her to any bother.

"Pizza's okay once in a while, but I try to get them to eat wholesome food whenever I can. I have leftover roast beef in the fridge. I'm thinking of hot roast beef sandwiches, if that's okay."

"That sounds fine. You really *do* try to be Super mom, don't you?"

She bristled a bit. "Is there something wrong with that?"

"No. Not if it doesn't wear you out."

Her shoulders relaxed. "It does. But as long as I can do it, I'm going to try."

They could hear the kids chattering as they trudged down the trail. They could see them. But David knew the trees blocked the kids' view of *them*. No one else had followed them into these rows of trees, and it almost felt as if they were alone in the middle of nowhere.

Angela was looking up at him with those big, blue eyes. He'd taken off his gloves after he'd cut down the tree so he could rope it to the sled. Now he was glad he had. Her swingy hair brushed against her cheek, and he pushed it back, letting his thumb linger on the softness of her skin. Her eyes grew bluer and wider, and he saw the same desire there that he was feeling. They were both wondering—wondering what a kiss would be like…wondering if a fire would start…wondering if the earth would move.

He rarely acted on impulse anymore. But now, desire drove him to seize the moment, answer some of his questions, discover if the chemistry he was feeling was real. When he bent his head, she raised her chin. His lips covered hers.

Did the kiss last for an instant? Or maybe an hour?

There *was* no time as heat exploded in his body…as he pushed his tongue into her mouth…as she responded quickly and fiercely.

When her children's laughter soared up the hill to

them, he broke away and stepped back, feeling turned inside out.

That was impossible. The kiss had begun and was over in a few seconds. How could he be so fully aroused? How could he want to lay her down in the pine needles and the patches of snow and take the passion she seemed willing to give?

He'd thought his questions would be answered after a kiss, but there were only more of them. "I shouldn't have done that. The way Anthony is feeling right now, if he senses anything going on between us, he'd never let me become his friend."

"You're right," she murmured. "And I'm not looking for…for…for an involvement. I don't have time. I don't have the energy. Men cause me nothing but disappointment." She brought her hand to her lips when she realized she'd said out loud what she was thinking.

"I'll try not to disappoint you where Anthony's concerned," he vowed solemnly. "Come on. We'd better catch up."

She didn't argue, and he knew she didn't want to linger, either. She'd obviously been hurt, maybe by someone other than her ex-husband. They both had scars that would keep anything from developing except a hot affair.

And it would be hot. That sample kiss had told him that.

But he *had* to put Anthony first.

He'd make sure he stayed away from Angela Schumacher. That was the only reasonable thing to do.

Chapter Three

Later Sunday evening when the doorbell rang, Angela was still reeling from David's kiss at the Christmas tree farm. It had practically knocked her boots off, yet she'd acted as if nothing had happened and he'd left after a quick supper. Now, for a change, all three kids were watching the same program on TV while she tidied up the empty ornament boxes.

When she opened her front door, she found Rebecca Peters. Rebecca was the newest neighbor on Danbury Way and Angela had liked her immediately. She was one of the most stylish women around, with gold highlights in her dark-brown hair, blue eyes and a very fashion-forward wardrobe.

She, too, had found romance.

"I thought you and Joe were away for the weekend."

"We didn't go. Joe couldn't find somebody to cover

for him at the clinic." Joe Hudson was a veterinarian and took his responsibility for his furry friends seriously.

"But…" Rebecca drawled, holding out her hand to Angela.

"It's beautiful!" Angela stared at the simply exquisite solitaire on Rebecca's finger, then gave her friend a huge hug. "This is wonderful. When are you getting married?"

Taking Rebecca by the hand, Angela tugged her toward the kitchen. "We'll have a cup of tea and you can tell me all about it."

Rebecca laughed as she followed Angela into the wine-and-spruce-green kitchen with its island in the middle, eat-on counter along one wall and numerous birch cabinets.

After another look at Rebecca's diamond under the brighter kitchen lights, Angela said, "I knew this would happen sooner rather than later."

"Me, too," Rebecca confided with a shy smile. "I love him to death. Since he had to go to the clinic, I told him I was going to come over and tell you our good news."

While Angela put on the tea kettle, Rebecca wiggled her hand under the recessed lighting. "We'll probably be planning the wedding for spring. I want the works—from wedding gown to flower girl."

They chatted for a few minutes about the type of gown Rebecca might choose, about colors she liked for her attendants, about possibilities for facilities for receptions.

The teakettle whistled, and Angela brought it over to the counter where she poured water into two mugs.

Adding the teabags, Rebecca admitted, "I really came over here to find out who that hunky man was in your driveway this afternoon."

"You weren't too busy to notice someone in my driveway?" Angela teased.

Although Rebecca's cheeks turned a little pinker, she admitted, "Joe and I can't spend *all* our time in bed."

Both women laughed. Then Angela sobered up quickly when she thought about David. He was going to pick up Anthony on Friday to take him to the movies. They'd settled that much. Actually, there wasn't anything else to settle, she told herself firmly.

"He's going to be Anthony's Big Brother, although Anthony still isn't sure he really wants one. We all went sledding yesterday, and then this afternoon we found a Christmas tree."

"Anthony's Big Brother," Rebecca mused. "Hmm. Are you sure that's all he's going to be?"

"He's younger than I am," Angela said lamely.

"How much younger?"

"Three years."

"That's nothing."

"Maybe."

"Is he single?"

"Oh, yes."

"What's he do?"

"He owns a sporting goods store in the same plaza as Felice's Nieces."

"This is David Moore we're talking about?" Rebecca asked, sounding concerned.

"Do you know him?"

Rebecca's blue eyes clouded. "No, I don't. But I've heard things."

Trepidation danced up Angela's spine. "What kind of things?"

"He's a football coach."

Angela nodded. "I know that."

After hesitating a few moments, Rebecca went on, "Now, I wasn't there, understand. The incident happened before I moved here. But he was involved in some kind of brawl on the football field and ended up with community service because of it."

Shocked, Angela leaned against the island. "You mean an actual physical fight?"

Rebecca nodded. "Yep, an actual fight between him and another coach."

"I don't understand. How could he keep his coaching position? Why would the community center put him on a list to be a mentor?"

"I don't know the ins and outs of it. How did Anthony relate to him?"

"By the time David left tonight, they were talking football. I think he's coming around. But now I don't know if I want David Moore around him."

"Maybe I shouldn't have said anything."

Rosewood was one of those communities where gossip spread like an epidemic. Their neighborhood was the perfect example. For a long while, Megan had been the butt of it. Everybody had thought her sister was sleeping with Carly's husband before Carly and Greg had broken up, which hadn't been true at all. Still, Rebecca didn't gossip idly, and a brawl on a football field would have had plenty of witnesses.

"I'm going to have to find out what this is all about," Angela decided soberly. She'd call David tomorrow and ask him to meet her for coffee. They'd get this straightened out one way or another.

Pushing her own concerns aside for the moment, she said to Rebecca, "Now tell me what you want Joe to wear for the wedding."

When Angela entered Rosewood's trendy coffee shop, Latte & Lunch, residents on their way to work or up early for whatever reason were drinking lattes, macchiatos and espressos. Angela hadn't had any caffeine yet so she couldn't blame her increased heart rate on that. She'd told herself this meeting with David could be a confrontation, and she was simply nervous.

Underneath that, there was something else and she couldn't deny it. She'd gone through the motions with him on Sunday evening as they'd decorated the tree and then had supper, all the while still tingling from their kiss at the Christmas tree farm.

Now the tingles were anticipatory ones and she simply didn't know how to shut them off.

He was waiting for her at a table for two in the corner. When he stood, his expression was serious. "I would have ordered for you, but I didn't know what you'd like."

She could see he was already nursing a cup of what looked like black coffee.

"I'll get something and be right back." Postponing the inevitable, she thought, not really wanting a cup of latte. But she needed something to do with her hands...something to focus on other than him.

Back at the table, the busyness of the place was almost a comfort because no one was paying attention to anyone else.

"Is this about that kiss?" he asked.

That kiss. She hadn't given him any indication on the

phone of why she wanted to meet. "No. I found something out and I thought we should talk about it."

"You found something out?"

She could feel her cheeks heating up. "I heard gossip—about you."

"I see. Want to fill me in?" His hazel eyes were steady on hers, not evading her, and she hoped Rebecca was all wrong about what she'd heard.

"One of my neighbors told me something that was disturbing to me. She said you were in a brawl on the football field while you were coaching."

Time ticked by as conversations and people swirled around them. "I see. The references I gave you didn't reassure you?"

"They reassured me when I didn't know about the fighting. But if you've got a temper, if you have anger that erupts like that, how can I trust you with Anthony?"

"Have you seen any sign of anger?" he asked. His voice was stiff and defensive.

"No, but that doesn't mean it isn't there. I've only been around you for two days. And men who have anger issues can sometimes keep them well hidden."

Looking down at his coffee, he turned it around in his hands. Then he met her gaze, his voice crisp. "What happened is a matter of public record. I'll admit, I was angry after my accident. My life had been torn apart and taken a turn I never expected. But I funneled that anger into recovery, into working in a lumber yard until I had enough money to buy my own store. While I did that, I coached."

"That one particular night, I was coaching a game and one of my players got clipped. The two boys started a fight. The other team's coach got involved, and so did I, shouting back and forth. In the midst of the ruckus, Coach Witherspoon turned on my player, who was mixing it up with his. I told him to move away, and he swung at me. I defended myself by swinging back. It wasn't the brightest thing I've ever done, but I felt I was defending my player."

Of course, this situation wasn't cut and dried. Angela sighed, not knowing what to think. Before her divorce she'd thought she was a good judge of character. David's demeanor toward the kids had told her he was kind and wouldn't fly off the handle at the drop of a hat. But she'd been wrong in so many ways about Jerome, and she could be wrong about this man, too.

David took her silence as a request for further information. "The chief of police was in the bleachers, and before either of us could throw another punch, he split up the fight. Since practically the whole community had seen what happened, Chief Raymond didn't feel he could let it drop. So he suggested we both do fifty hours of community service, mentoring needy kids. That's how I got into the program."

"That coach shouldn't have been mentoring kids if he couldn't keep his temper in check. What was the chief thinking?" Angela asked, outraged.

"He was thinking that sports can sometimes bring out the worst, as well as the best. He was thinking we'd both gotten caught up in the moment, as well as the players. Witherspoon isn't a bad guy. I got to know him afterwards. He should never have swung in the first place. And I should never have swung back, no question about it."

She liked the fact David was taking responsibility for what had happened.

"I can't speak for Witherspoon," David continued. "I can only tell you about me. I was twenty-three then and trying to find my way. I've learned a lot in five years, and my life has stabilized. I've kept mentoring kids all that time and not one of them, or their parents, has had a complaint. Other than the references I gave you, you can go to the community center files to check out the recommendations and reports yourself. Most of all, I think you should look at the man I am today, rather than the man I used to be."

"I don't *know* who you are today."

"You're a parent, and you don't want to take anybody else's word for it. I get that. All I can say is that experience taught me the kids should come first. I think I've learned that lesson well. But you're going to have to take it all into consideration and then make your decision. Anthony's your son and you don't want him around anyone who wouldn't be the best influence."

Another man might have gotten angry with her because she had listened to gossip. But she could see David wasn't angry. He'd removed himself from her, though. The lights of desire she'd seen in his eyes were gone. To her surprise he wasn't trying to convince her to think his way, the way Jerome often had and still did. He was letting the facts stand for themselves and allowing her to make the decision.

The thing was, staring into his hazel eyes, feeling the tug of attraction for him even now, she couldn't make the decision. "I have to think about all of this."

David stood, towering over her. "You think about it. The community center can find you another mentor for Anthony, but I want you to remember something. Hard experiences can lead to change, and I've changed my life into something I like now. Give me a call if you want me to take Anthony to the movies on Friday." Taking a business card from his pocket, he laid it on the table next to her coffee. "My cell phone number is on there if you need it."

Then he left the restaurant, leaving Angela feeling… empty.

On Wednesday afternoon, David was explaining the benefits of the Alpina cross-country skis to a customer when the phone on the cashier's desk rang and his manager picked it up.

"It's for you," Edgar Pawalski said. "An emergency."

After excusing himself from the customer, letting Edgar take over, David picked up the receiver, trying not to panic. His dad lived alone at the farm and anything could happen.

Instead, he heard a high-pitched woman's voice. "Coach Moore? I understand you're a Big Brother to Anthony Buffington?"

Immediately David was taken back to his conversation with Angela the day before yesterday. He'd been unsettled by the fact that she couldn't seem to put her faith in him, and he hadn't completely analyzed why. He'd hoped he'd hear from Angela, but he hadn't, though he hadn't heard from the community center, either. He was sure he would have if Angela had told them she wanted another mentor.

"Yes, I'm Anthony's Big Brother."

"This is the principal of Rosewood Elementary School. I'm in a bit of a pickle. Anthony was playing basketball after school. He fell and injured his arm, but I can't get hold of his mother or his father. He says he has an aunt, but she's away on a business trip. He's in a lot of pain. When I asked him who else he might want me to call, he mentioned you."

That surprised David. "You can't reach Ms. Schumacher?" That seemed unbelievable to him because Angela would always be available for her kids. "Have you tried Felice's Nieces?"

"Anthony told us she works part-time there, and we're wondering if her cell phone isn't charged or if she might have turned it off in transit. He's pretty miserable and upset. Maybe you could come talk to him until we can reach her? Nothing we say seems to help."

"How badly is he hurt?"

"I'm no doctor, Coach, but I've seen lots of accidents with kids and I think his arm is broken."

"I'll be right there."

"Come to the nurse's office at the elementary school. You'll have to stop in at the main office first to get clearance."

"Will do."

Ten minutes later David had stopped in the elementary school office, spoken to the secretary, and was walking down the corridor to the nurse's office. He was familiar with the ins and outs of the high school since he coached there. He'd been to the elementary school gym on a few occasions, but had never entered the recesses of the school itself. Normally, the pictures hanging on the cork strips outside the classrooms would make him smile. With Christmas coming, craft projects seemed to abound—from Christmas trees decorated with popcorn balls to reindeer fashioned from paper plates. But he was too worried about Anthony to appreciate the whimsy of the art projects.

When he entered the nurse's office, he saw Anthony hunched up in a corner of the cot against the wall. The nurse was sitting at her desk at a computer.

He rapped on the door. "I'm David Moore," he told the nurse before she could get up.

"Oh, Coach Moore. I just reached Ms. Schumacher. She's on her way."

"Mom's gonna be *so* mad," Anthony mumbled, his eyes filling with tears. He was cradling his arm and David went over to sit beside him.

"Why would she be mad? It's not your fault you fell."

"She didn't want me to stay tonight because she was working. She said it would be easier for Zooey if I just came home with Olivia and Michael. But I wanted to stay, and she let me, and now she can't even work 'cause she has to come get me. She's going to be mad."

Not knowing how much comfort Anthony would want, yet following his instincts, he capped the boy's shoulder. "She's not going to be mad. She's going to be worried. All she's going to care about is that you're okay."

"But I'm not. I have to go to the hospital."

At that moment, Angela rushed into the nurse's office and came up short when she saw David.

"Anthony asked them to call me when they couldn't get hold of you," he said in quiet explanation.

"I forgot to charge my phone last night. When I got to Felice's Nieces, there was a message to call the school."

David moved away as she rushed over to Anthony and

put her arm around him. "Oh, honey. How are you doing?"

"It hurts, Mom."

David could see the boy was trying to keep a stiff upper lip for his mother, but it wasn't working too well. He went on, "I'm sorry I fell. I shouldn't have stayed. If I had listened to you—"

"It's okay," she said soothingly. "The important thing now is to get you taken care of."

It was easy to see how upset Angela was, even though she was trying to hide it. Her hand was shaking a bit, and David didn't think she should drive Anthony herself. "Would you like me to drive you to the emergency room?"

Angela's gaze met his and they both remembered the last conversation they had. "I can't ask you to do that."

"You don't have to ask. I'm offering. I think it would be safer for everyone if I drove."

She took a deep, calming breath. "I hate to admit it, but I think you're right. The problem is, I won't have my van when we're all finished."

"I can drive your van and then get a ride back here."

Her blue eyes asked the question if he was trying to prove she was wrong about him…wrong to doubt him. But that wasn't why he was doing this. Something about Angela more than interested him. She was trying to take on the world, all by herself, and take care of her kids at the same time. She deserved a little help.

The nurse got up from her chair then. "We keep a wheelchair here just for these kinds of situations. I can wheel Anthony outside."

"If you give me your keys I'll bring your van to the front door," David said to Angela.

After only a moment's hesitation, she reached into her purse and took out her key ring. About ten keys were on a ring attached to a large rhinestone star. He had to smile.

Fifteen minutes later they were at the hospital. Angela had called the pediatrician, and he'd advised her to take Anthony to the emergency room. An hour had passed until Angela filled out the paperwork and an orthopedic doctor had checked out Anthony, who had insisted David come to the examining room with them.

The doctor told Angela, "I need X-rays. I'll send someone for your son. Do you want to come along?"

"Can Coach Moore come instead?" Anthony asked the doctor.

Angela's hurt was evident in the quick sheen that coated her eyes. "You don't want me to come with you?"

"Oh, Mom, you'll just cry or somethin'. Coach Moore is probably used to this kind of thing, playing sports and all." He looked up at David. "Did you have X-rays after your accident?"

"I had all kinds of tests."

"See? I told you, Mom."

Her attention went from her son to David. "Do you mind?"

"Not at all. While we're gone, you can take a few deep breaths. I doubt if we'll be long."

Once the attendant came to wheel Anthony to X-ray, the rest didn't take long at all. David kept the boy distracted as best he could, telling him about playing football in high school and college, asking Anthony what subjects he liked best in school, discovering the boy intended to be a firefighter when he grew up. The arm was hurting him badly. David could tell. Talking seemed to help, and by the time the attendant wheeled Anthony back to the cubicle in the E.R., they were on their way to forming a friendship of sorts. That was going to be all shot to hell if Angela decided she wanted another mentor for her son. But Anthony needed a friend now, and David could be that for him tonight.

Waiting wasn't anybody's strong suit, and by the time the doctor reported to Angela what the X-rays had shown, David could see she was worried sick but trying to pretend she was a competent mother who took accidents like this in stride.

The doctor was all business as he declared, "It's broken, all right. We might as well take care of setting it now. No use making the boy suffer longer than he has to. Son, have you had anything to eat this afternoon?"

"No, sir. Nothing since lunch."

"Great. We'll get you prepped and you can go home with a cast that everybody can sign."

Things moved fast after that. Before they knew it, Angela was kissing Anthony, and a nurse was wheeling him away. She'd followed the gurney out of the cubicle and stood in the hall looking after it.

David picked up the bag that held Anthony's clothes and belongings. "Come on. Let's go up to the waiting room outside same-day surgery. The doctor said that's where they'll bring him when he's finished."

When she turned toward him, she was pale.

"He's going to be all right," David reassured her.

"I know. But he's so little. The hospital's so big. I don't want him to be scared. I don't want this to hurt his chances to be anything he wants to be."

"Nothing's going to keep that boy down."

She ducked her head and David knew why. Taking her hand, he pulled her back into the cubicle for some privacy. Setting the bag of clothes on a vinyl chair, he cupped her chin in his hand and lifted her head. Tears were streaming down her cheeks.

"What's wrong?" he asked gently.

"I tried to do everything right. I married a man I thought I could have a life with. We were happy with three beautiful kids until I found out about his affairs. Until he decided he wanted to be single. Until everything fell apart. I don't know what I would have done without Megan the past three years. But she's moving out, I had to take this extra job, and now Anthony's hurt. And I can't get in touch with Jerome. It's as if he doesn't even *care* he has a family. Or *had* a family. Somehow I always feel as if everything is all my fault."

Her tears were flowing in earnest now, and there was only one thing David could do. He enfolded her into his arms.

Holding Angela was supposed to be a comfort-giving gesture. She needed someone to lean on, and he was there. She *was* leaning into him. Her breasts were pressing into his chest. Her sweet, summer-garden scent filled his nostrils and made him need in elemental ways. Her hair was silky under his jaw as he held her and she cried out of frustration, loss and fear. He suspected there was a lot of fear. She was a woman alone with three kids. She could be afraid of responsibility and bills and a life that was changing. At first, she'd seemed to be the epitome of an independent woman, and maybe she was. But this was another side of her—the side that needed a man's comfort and support and a shoulder that was strong enough to help get her through this crisis.

Who was the real Angela? Did she want to be on her own? Did she want to hook up with a man? Did she need someone to count on? Or was she looking for an easier way to live her life than as a single mom?

Jessica had had a poor background without the loving family David had experienced in his early years. She'd worked at a fitness center, but as they'd gotten engaged and they'd both pinned their hopes on NFL dreams, she'd talked about quitting her job, searching for a house for them, taking the time to decorate it and join a few clubs. She'd wanted a life with him that would lift her out of the one she'd known. Not so much emotionally, but physically and monetarily. He hadn't realized all that until after she'd left.

He wouldn't be any woman's easy way out again.

Angela's sobs had ebbed away and she was quiet now, just resting against him. Freezing the desire that raced through him like a running back heading for a touchdown, he forced himself to put his hands on her shoulders and back away.

When she looked up at him, there was confusion there...and dismay. "I'm so sorry. I don't break down like this. It's not me."

Was that the truth? he wondered. Was this situation with Anthony the clincher after a long list of squalls she'd had to handle on her own? "Don't worry about it," he said. "You're entitled. Your son was just taken to the operating room."

Seeing the bag of Anthony's belongings on the chair, she went to it. "I tossed my purse in here." Retrieving it, she straightened her shoulders. "I'm going to the ladies' room before we head upstairs. I know you're probably sorry you got mixed up in this whole thing. I never meant to fall apart on you." She ran her hand through her hair. "I must look a mess."

"You couldn't look a mess if you tried," he said honestly.

At that, color came back into her cheeks again. "I'll meet you in the E.R. waiting room in five minutes, tops. I promise."

As Angela went down the corridor, he realized he'd have to decide just how involved he wanted to get in her life.

Then again, maybe getting involved wasn't an option. He didn't even know if she still wanted a mentor for her son. He wondered if he should *be* that mentor—or if he should walk away now.

When Angela saw the luxury sedan pull into her driveway the following evening, she didn't know what to think. Then she saw David climb out of the passenger side, another tall, broad-shouldered man get out of the driver's side.

Her first inclination was to run and hide. She'd felt like an absolute idiot since David had comforted her in the hospital. All throughout her marriage she'd been strong. Throughout her breakup with Jerome she'd been strong. Throughout the settlement talks and the whole divorce she'd been strong. During the past three years since the divorce she'd been strong. What had happened yesterday in that emergency room cubicle had been out of character for her. Stress was a constant companion and she knew how to deal with it. She worked, she went about her life, she took care of her kids, and she had the confidence she could overcome anything. But working two jobs, having less time with her kids, needing to make excuses for Jerome and seeing Anthony hurt had finally gotten to her.

What must David Moore think of her? The bigger question was, why did it matter? He'd been the perfect gentleman after she fell apart. He'd waited around, reading less-than-current magazines with her in the waiting room. He'd driven her and Anthony home in her car and called a friend to pick him up. She'd thanked him more than once, and he'd brushed that off. With her attention on her still-groggy son, she'd put David in the worry-about-it-later category, subconsciously never expecting to see him again.

Yet, here he was. And she knew why. He was concerned about Anthony.

She wasn't a diehard fan of football, but she knew the game, as well as the important players. Immediately she recognized Duke Smith and realized David had brought him to see Anthony.

Bored to death, killing time until tomorrow when he could go back to school with his friends, her son had been spending most of his time in his room. What would he say when he saw Duke Smith?

She opened her door to the two men, not knowing quite how to act. But introductions took the awkwardness from the moment.

She pumped the defensive linebacker's hand, a little starstruck herself. "It's so good to meet you. I never expected David might bring you by."

Duke's nose looked as if it had been broken. There was a bump on it. But it fit well on his strong-jawed face. He was as tall as David but huskier. "I happened to be in town visiting. I was in New York for a meeting yesterday and called David to see if he wanted to catch up. He told me about your boy."

"Anthony called me this morning," David told Angela. "Did you know that?"

She shook her head. "No, he didn't tell me. I hope he's not bothering you."

"No bother. But I didn't know if you wanted me here. So I figured if Duke came along maybe we could raise his spirits a little. He seemed pretty down. I told him he's lucky it's his left arm."

She wanted to address the subject of David being Anthony's mentor, but she didn't want to do it in front of Duke.

"He's up in his room. Michael's there, too, probably bugging him."

"Olivia's not around?" David asked.

"No, she's over at a friend's."

"This is a nice neighborhood." Duke motioned outside to the cul-de-sac. "I just bought my first house. A place in Virginia. It's a weird feeling, being a homeowner. Now I have to worry about rain and snow and mowing grass."

She laughed. "Do you have much grass?"

"An acre. And I have a pool. Don't know how much I'll get to use it, but I liked the idea when I saw the place."

With a quick glance at David, she noticed the shadows on his face. Was he thinking about what he might have had? Was he thinking about losing the chance of being the landowner of a country estate? Having all the trimmings Duke now enjoyed?

"Having a home is a huge responsibility. There always seems to be something to do or fix or add," she sympathized.

Suddenly Michael called from Anthony's bedroom. "Mom, Anthony's being mean to me."

Angela shook her head. "Do you want me to announce you? Or do you want to surprise them?"

"Surprise is always the best offense," David said with a smile.

She motioned toward the steps. "Then be my guests."

When Duke moved forward, she caught David's arm. He was wearing a football jersey, and the muscles under her fingers were tough and taut and all-man. "Can I talk to you for a few minutes in private before you leave?"

"Sure." His grin was gone now. "I'll make sure we get the chance."

She could feel the heat of his skin. She could feel the heat of *him*.

Then he pulled away and she had to ask herself, did she want to talk to him for Anthony's sake...or her own?

Chapter Four

"Look, Mom. Duke signed my cast! Isn't it awesome? He even drew a football."

After giving the men a half hour with Anthony and Michael, Angela had come upstairs to rescue them. She didn't want them to think they had to stay all night. The two boys could tie them up forever with their questions.

"It's Mr. Smith," she reminded her son.

"Everybody calls me Duke," David's friend assured her with a grin. "I don't mind. I've just been telling your boy how I keep in shape." He motioned to David. "Now *he* can tell you about the real nitty-gritty of building muscle. After his accident he was in rehab for a month, then outpatient workouts for three more."

David's slight shake of his head told Duke he didn't want to get into all that. Because it had ruined his career? Or for some other reason? Something had given David his compassion, his maturity, his ability to be strong and steady when someone needed him.

Now, don't be thinking there's a man who can be dependable, she warned herself. Because she knew better.

Michael came over to Angela and looked up at her. "I'm hungry, Mom. Are we gonna' eat soon?"

"In about fifteen minutes. I have enough pot roast if the two of you would like to stay."

"Sorry, we can't," Duke said. "We're going to a party tonight in the city."

David's expression was bland, and Angela wondered if going to a party in the city was no big deal for him. Maybe he did it often. After all, he was an eligible bachelor.

"A party in New York City?" Anthony asked. "Will other football players be there?"

With a grin, Duke nodded. "Yep. Some of my teammates. But lots of other people will be there, too."

Lots of women, Angela thought. She could just picture them—tall svelte models, professional women who were stockbrokers, lawyers and anything else they wanted to be. She was sure David and Duke could have their pick.

"Maybe I can get a few autographs for you boys," David offered.

"You'd do that?" Anthony asked, and Angela's heart hurt a little because Jerome never went out of his way for his kids. These two strangers had done more for Anthony's morale than Jerome had done in the past three years.

A buzzer sounded in the kitchen. "I have to take something out of the oven," she explained. Crossing to her son, she leaned down and whispered, "Don't forget to thank

Duke and Coach Moore for coming." Then she exited the room to let the boys say their final goodbyes.

Down in the kitchen, she found her potholders and removed the baked apples from the oven, setting them on a rack on the counter. Unfortunately, she might not get a chance to talk to David alone tonight. She didn't want to say what she had to say in front of Duke, and if they were going to a party—

"Something smells good," David said from the doorway.

"It's the cinnamon and brown sugar."

His smile was easy, but his eyes were serious as he went on, "Michael's showing Duke his trucks, so I thought we'd have a few minutes."

Suddenly tongue-tied, she hurriedly expressed her gratitude. "I don't know how to thank you for everything you did, taking Anthony to the hospital and all."

"I told you yesterday no thanks are necessary."

When he came toward the kitchen island, she moved closer to him, already feeling the pull of attraction she'd experienced since the day she'd met him. "I think Anthony's beginning to like you, maybe even trust you. I wondered if you still want to be his mentor, in spite of my…doubts."

"That depends. Do you still have doubts?"

How could she explain this without giving too much personal history? "You've got to understand something. My ability to trust a man has been shaken more than once. But I don't think you could relate to Anthony and the kids the way you have, if you didn't have kindness in you. The community center doesn't lightly put anyone on their Big Brother list. I checked with Chief of Police Raymond and he confirmed your story was true."

"My word wasn't enough?" David appeared troubled.

"No, it wasn't. I had to be sure, where my kids were concerned. I don't know you, David, any more than you know me. I do understand about past mistakes, though. Maybe better than lots of people. I've certainly made enough of my own. I see how Anthony's connecting with you, and I'm hoping you can build on that and give him the self esteem he's been lacking. This is all about *him,*" she declared, relaying the message that anything between them was inconsequential compared to the welfare of her son.

He laid one hand on the island, close to her hip. She noticed again how large it was…how strong he looked.

"I think you're right about Anthony's self-esteem," David responded. "Your ex-husband has made him feel that he's not worthy of his love. A friendship with me won't replace what's missing, but I'm hoping it will make him feel better about himself."

This man got it, and that impressed her. Coaching had taught him what made kids tick. "Michael told me the kids were impressed that you're Anthony's Big Brother. They respect you."

"As long as the team keeps winning," he joked with a self-deprecating laugh. "I have no illusions about that. But coaches do carry a bit of clout. Duke Smith carries even more. Once Anthony's classmates discover he met him, they'll all want to be his friend."

The mention of Duke brought to mind his car in her driveway and the party the two of them were going to attend in the city. "So you're going to a party tonight?"

"Not a party, exactly. A get-together."

"Are you staying over?"

"Duke is. I'm not. Too much going on with the store at Christmas. Do you want me to stop in again tomorrow night? I could play a board game or something with Anthony."

"That would be great. I'm sending him to school tomorrow, but it could be a frustrating day. He clams up with me, but he might talk to you."

Suddenly Duke appeared in the kitchen doorway. "Ready to go?"

"Sure am."

"It was nice meeting you, Angela." Duke sounded as if he meant it.

"Thank you for stopping by. It meant a lot to my son."

After a last, long look, David followed Duke to the front door.

Angela heard it close. She heard the big car drive away and wished her sister were home so she could talk to her. Checking her watch, she picked up the cordless phone and dialed Megan's cell. Her sister's voice mail picked up.

Angela settled the phone in its base, feeling stranded somehow and not exactly sure why.

"They're watching a movie," Zooey told Angela the following evening, as Angela set her purse on the counter and shrugged out of her coat. "Coach Moore said he stopped by now because he has to go back to the store tonight," Zooey added. "He wanted to keep his word to Anthony. He brought him autographs that you should probably frame!" Zooey's eyes were big with questions and her voice held curiosity.

"I'm glad he kept his word," Angela replied. "Not many men do that anymore."

"Don't you forget Jack. He always does what he says he's going to do."

Angela grinned. "Of course I can't forget Jack. He's absolutely perfect."

Her neighbor wrinkled her nose at her. "Emily and Olivia are upstairs. Do you want me to take Emily home?" Zooey was already gathering up Jack Jr., who had a cookie in his hand and crumbs all over the front of his shirt.

"She's welcome to stay for supper. You know that."

"Send her home afterward. Jack and I are taking the kids Christmas shopping in the city tomorrow. This might be a disaster of the worst kind."

"No, it won't. If worse comes to worst, you just won't buy any presents. You'll have fun."

Minutes later Zooey had bundled up Jack Jr. and herself and they were out the door. Angela was grateful for having such a good friend who was willing to fill in until Megan returned. She didn't know what she was going to do with the kids in the new year. Maybe she'd have to enroll them in the after-school program.

Before she went to the family room, she called up the steps. "I'm home."

Coming into the hall, Olivia called back, "Can Emily stay for supper?"

"She sure can."

Olivia disappeared into her room again.

At the doorway to the family room, Angela saw Anthony and Michael were engrossed in a DVD. It looked like a comedy with lots of animals. After a smile at David, she asked the boys, "How was school?"

"Okay," they both mumbled, still paying attention to the movie.

David rose from the sofa and went to her. "I think they like that one," he said with a smile.

"Did Anthony say how his day went?"

"I think it was rough. And he's tired. He can hardly keep his eyes open. Handling his backpack and books and everything with one arm couldn't have been easy. He does have new names on his cast, though, so the day couldn't have been all bad."

"Would you like a cup of coffee? Zooey said you have to get back to the store tonight."

They were having idle conversation on one level, but on another, his eyes held hers. Her breath quickened, and she knew offering him coffee would give her a few minutes to talk to him alone. What could happen in a few minutes?

"A cup of coffee sounds great. I do have to get back to the store to check in some new inventory," he repeated as he followed her into the kitchen. "I'm going to be off tomorrow."

She didn't know whether to nudge for more information or not. Instead of prying, she asked, "How was the party?"

"It was fun. Duke's life is very different from mine now, so our friends are different, too."

"Meaning?" she asked, wondering what he was trying to tell her.

"Meaning, at one time a penthouse party and staying out all night would have suited my lifestyle just fine. Now that's just not the case."

After she took a filter from the cupboard, she removed

the coffee from the refrigerator and scooped in a pot's worth. Then she filled the tank in the back. All the while, she was aware of David watching her. She felt a bit self-conscious, yet there was some feminine satisfaction in having his eyes on her. A thrill skipped through her because he seemed to be attracted to her as much as she was attracted to him. Not that that would get them anywhere.

"If this question's too personal, you don't have to answer it." She switched on the coffee pot. "What kind of accident were you in?"

His jaw set a bit. A shadow passed over his features that told her this wasn't something he spoke about often, and he might not talk about it now.

"You said you were in training when it happened?" she prompted.

"I was in training, but it didn't have anything to do with that."

She knew she must look puzzled.

They were both standing near the island now, David around the corner from her. "After I went to training camp, I became friends with Duke and another player, Travis Dodson. The three of us were tight right away. We just connected."

"Friends without knowing exactly why," she interjected so he'd know she understood.

"Exactly. Maybe it was where we came from, maybe it was just our temperament. I don't know. A few weeks after training started the area had torrential thunderstorms. We were on one of the main highways. Because of the storm, cars hydroplaned. A driver crossed the median line and crashed into us. Travis was driving and died on impact.

Miraculously, Duke wasn't harmed. But my leg was broken, my knee injured, and I had some internal injuries. I didn't need the doctors to tell me my football career had ended that night."

"I'm so sorry that happened to you." She wanted to take his hand, hold his arm, give him a hug. But after kissing him, she knew she couldn't do any of those things. There was too much steam between them, too much sexual tension that could blaze out of control.

"Having Travis die that way, being in the car with him—I was conscious the whole time—was worse than everything else. When the therapist told me I could rehabilitate my body again, I felt guilty doing it for a while because Travis hadn't had that chance. Rehab was hell. It was just something I had to get through. After a while I was doing it for Travis, as well as myself. That might sound crazy—"

"It doesn't sound crazy at all. What about Duke? How did he feel after the accident?"

"He went through a real bad time. He couldn't understand why he hadn't been harmed…why he only had bruises when his friend was dead and I was cracked up pretty badly. But he was there as often as he could be, cheering me on, not letting me give up. He's a good friend."

"And you've stayed friends." That in itself told Angela Duke wasn't merely feeling guilty, that he and David had genuine bonds that had lasted all these years. "I can see how an experience like you had could change a person."

His hazel eyes holding hers, he offered, "It made me understand what was important in life."

"What is important?" She knew what was important to her and for some reason needed to know how his priorities stacked up.

"Good friends. Building a future. Earning success. Tell me something. Did your divorce change you?"

"I'm sure it did. It's made me more independent, more furiously protective of my children. As I mentioned, we tried to keep it amicable, but I was bitter. I'll admit it."

"Your ex-husband was unfaithful?"

She had spilled that to him the day Anthony had broken his arm. "Yes. And not just once. When I finally opened my eyes, I couldn't accept what our relationship had become. Marriage was supposed to be about sharing, but we didn't share anything. Sure, we were parents with kids. But Jerome didn't take that seriously. Even before we divorced, he popped in and out of their lives, was never around when it counted so they could depend on him."

"So you had the full burden of being a parent even then."

"I guess I did. Fortunately, I have good friends on Danbury Way, and I don't know what I would have done without my sister Megan."

"When does she get home?"

"I'm hoping on Sunday."

After studying her for a few moments, he said, "I'm taking off tomorrow to go home to my dad's farm. How would you and the kids like to go along?"

The invitation was totally unexpected and threw her off balance. "Oh, I don't know. With Christmas coming I have a million things to do. I have to work in the morning…" Her voice trailed off as she turned over the possibility in her mind.

"If you want to go, I can wait until afternoon to leave. We'd be on the road for about an hour. Since Anthony can't do his usual activities, he's probably going to be bored. And if he's bored—"

"He'll make life miserable for all of us," she verified with a small laugh.

She *should* say no to David. Yet they both knew what they had to do. They both knew they couldn't get involved and have David's friendship with Anthony work. Her son needed something she couldn't give him, and this outing could be a bright spot for all of them. It might even give her a little perspective on what she was going to do with her life after Megan moved out—how she was going to handle all her responsibilities and finances. Here, lately, she was reminded constantly she was hanging on by the edge of her teeth. An afternoon of relaxation sounded good for her, too, as well as for the kids.

"If you're sure we wouldn't be intruding, the outing sounds like a great idea. But what's your dad going to think if you descend on him with all of us?"

"My dad will welcome some life in the house again. The truth is, we don't have much to say to each other. These visits are sometimes more perfunctory than enjoyable. I think he'd love having the kids around. He's always complaining my sister doesn't visit enough with hers. But I should prepare you, he's a little grumpy sometimes and has definite opinions on everything."

"As a parent should."

David laughed. "As long as you go into it with that in mind, you two will get along fine."

Being around David's dad could be good for her kids. They didn't have grandparents who were accessible.

Jerome's mom and dad had divorced when he was a teenager. His mom lived in Europe and his dad in Oregon. Her dad wrote about once a year from wherever he and his wife happened to be. Her mom…

Angela always felt a twist in her chest when she thought of her mother. The divorce had changed her drastically and she'd turned from a loving, caring mother to one who had separated herself from her daughters. Everything had changed when Angela's parents divorced, and it had affected Megan almost more than her, because Megan had been adopted.

"I think a trip to a dairy farm and visiting with your dad could be just what the kids and I need." She went to the pot to pour two mugs of coffee, looking forward to the next day…looking forward to spending more time with David.

Angela knew the outing was a mistake as soon as she climbed into her van with David driving. It wasn't a mistake for her kids, but rather a mistake because she simply couldn't control her physical reactions around him. She'd never had a problem with blushing. Or tingling. Or heating up. Until that day in Felice's Nieces when he'd introduced himself. *Before* he'd introduced himself. Now for the first time in her life as a mother, she was glad for the raucous talking of her kids, the near fights, the jabs and "let-me-alones."

If she and David were alone now…

He was driving her van, simply because it had more room and they could all be comfortable. He'd thrown his jacket into the third seat next to Olivia who was in her own world, reading a Junie B. Jones chapter book. The boys had settled down, too. And that wasn't good because she had too much time to glance at David.

Her eyes seemed irrationally drawn to him. He was wearing a blue plaid flannel shirt over a navy T-shirt. The sleeves were rolled back on his forearms and the brown blond hair there gave her a shivery feeling inside whenever she looked at it. His jeans were worn, lighter blue at the knees and…and other places she tried not to let snag her attention. Whatever was wrong with her had better pass soon. Maybe her PMS had taken a sharp turn from moodiness to an increased sex drive.

Who was she kidding? Whatever PMS she'd ever had was due to *real* problems, not hormones. She'd never considered herself all that sexual. It had always been easy for her to be monogamous.

Unlike her ex-husband.

Try as she might, she attempted to keep her gaze away from David's large hands on the steering wheel. She wasn't having much luck at that, either.

When they'd left, the sky had been blue, but over the past hour as they'd driven north, gray clouds had skittered in. Now the blue was gone.

Earlier, David had finally found a radio station they could all agree on, and she hadn't had to worry about talking. Now, however, he switched it off. "We're almost there. About ten minutes." There were no other cars on the two-lane road and he studied the sky. "Looks like we could get some weather."

"And I don't have four-wheel drive," she said worriedly. "Maybe we should have brought your SUV."

"No use second-guessing ourselves now."

That was a huge difference between them. She second-guessed herself all the time—with everything that had had to do with her marriage, with her relationship with her mother, with what happened with the kids. Megan had been the same before she'd met Greg Banning. Now she seemed to have personal confidence, too, which Angela had always wished *she'd* possessed.

As the van climbed up a rise, she felt David glance at her. "What?" she asked, turning toward him.

"You worry a lot, don't you?"

"I'm a mom. Of course I worry a lot. I want to control the world."

He laughed. "At least you're honest about it."

"When you have kids," she explained, lowering her voice, "everything in your life changes. I don't wake up in the morning without thinking about them. I don't go to sleep at night without thinking about them. Since I think, I worry. I want everything to be perfect for them. And if not perfect, at least problem free. As young as Olivia is, there are cliques in her grade. I worry she'll be hurt by them. At five, Michael makes his sixes and his threes backward. Could he have a problem with dyslexia? And then Anthony—" She stopped. "It's not just school, it's everything. I'm a mom. It's what I do. But you couldn't begin to understand that. Not as a bachelor. Not as a man who's still free of responsibilities."

"You make me sound like a college kid who doesn't know a glass ceiling from a walk in the park. I own my own business, Angela. I coach kids. I know what problems are."

Not forgetting what he'd told her about rehab and the hell it was, his whole recovery process, she knew he understood overcoming obstacles. Still, being a parent was different. "As a single man, you have you, yourself and you to think about. I not only worry about Olivia's, Michael's and Anthony's everyday life, but their future happiness. Parenthood is big, David. Bigger than anything I've ever experienced on my own. I truly believe if anyone told a prospective parent what being a mom or dad was like, they wouldn't have kids."

Silent for a few moments, he finally replied, "But you had three."

"What's that old saying? In for a penny, in for a pound? The first child makes you think that having the second one couldn't be any harder. But then having the second one is totally different. Having two makes you think you're experienced. You could sleepwalk through a third. What a load of bunk!"

"And the *real* reason for two and three?" he asked with more perception than she'd expected.

She could feel herself blushing again, and she might as well get used to it, as long as David was within five feet of her. "I loved being a mom. From the moment Anthony was born, I knew I was made to do it. Does that sound totally New-Age freaky, or what?"

"It sounds as if you know who you are."

Oh, she knew who she was. She was a woman who shouldn't be looking at a man as if he were a centerfold model. She was a woman who was old enough to know better than to think having sex could add excitement to her life, rather than problems. She was a woman who knew having three children was one of the most important jobs in the world. No matter what David had experienced in his life, no single man his age would happily want to take on three kids.

What was she thinking? She shouldn't even be considering David Moore in the same sentence with family...
her family...her.

"There's the sign." He motioned to the placard that
looked as if it were growing out of long, tall weeds. Cloverleaf Dairy Farm. As he made a left turn, they moved
off of the paved road onto gravel.

"Hold on to your teeth," he warned the kids. "Some
of these potholes are as big as the Grand Canyon."

"That's *big*," Michael decided, peering out the window
to see if he could catch sight of any of them.

Anthony nudged him. "He doesn't *really* mean the
Grand Canyon. He just means they're huge. Won't they
hurt the van?" Anthony asked.

"Not if I can help it," David mumbled as he zigzagged
around one.

Living in the 'burbs all her life, Angela was used to
planned communities, streets with cookie-cutter houses,
a particular number of residences on a block with a mani-
cured lawn for each parcel. Even on Danbury Way, the
Colonial-style houses were basically alike, except for
Carly's mansion, which was designed to look like an old
plantation house and took two lots at the head of the cul-
de-sac. But even that had drywall under the wallpaper, the
latest energy-efficient windows and doors and two state-
of-the-art furnaces. Now, as Angela spotted the farmhouse, she was taken back in time.

"How old is the house?" She stared at the white, clap-
board two-story with its wraparound porch and black
shutters, as if it had many stories to tell.

"It's almost a hundred years old. It has those wide

windowsills and thick walls that help insulate it in both winter and summer. I keep telling dad he should replace the windows, but he keeps adding weather stripping. I did caulk them for him last year."

She stared at the house that looked as if it had at least two double-pane windows in every room.

"We refinished the windows last summer. It gave me something to do with him when I took some time off. We also have a tradition of painting two sides of the house every year. That way we never have to do the whole thing at once. We've done that since I was a kid. The barn's state-of-the-art, though. A fire destroyed most of the old one about ten years ago. Lightning hit it. We were lucky we didn't lose any livestock."

He said "we" as if he was still invested in this place. Or else he just wanted to keep it in tip-top shape for his dad. Either way, she admired him for it.

"There are chickens," Olivia called to the front. "Real live chickens! Can we go look at them?"

"As you can tell, my kids have been animal deprived."

"We want a dog," Anthony told David, "but Mom says it wouldn't be fair to the dog because we're away from the house so much."

"My dad has a dog. A yellow lab."

"Wow. A dog and chickens, too." Michael was beside himself with excitement and raring to get out and look at all of it.

"Before we see anything, we're going to meet Mr. Moore. Now remember your manners."

"We have to say please and thank you," Michael reminded Olivia and Anthony.

His brother just frowned at the idea of having to be on his best behavior.

After Angela unfastened her seat belt, so did the kids, and they all got out. Michael led Olivia and Anthony up onto the porch, but before Angela could take the first step, David clasped her arm.

She'd avoided touching him since their kiss. She'd avoided standing too close. She'd avoided prolonged eye contact. But now his hand was on her arm, and he was close enough that the puff of white air when he spoke almost mingled with her breath. His eyes held hers and the earth rocked.

"What?" she asked, feeling suddenly oxygen-deprived.

"Just so you know before we go in, my dad and I have differences."

She cocked her head, not understanding. "What kind of differences?"

"That's not important. But if he seems a little belligerent and I seem a little removed, that's why. I just thought you should know."

David had meant his words to be a warning of sorts, but now she was intrigued. Why would he and his dad be at odds? What had caused it? More importantly, would she and the kids be in the middle of it?

Chapter Five

David's father opened his front door and took a long look at his son. Then he turned his attention to Angela and the kids. "David told me he was bringing company." He held out his hand to her. "I'm Aaron Moore."

"You have chickens," Michael exploded.

"Can we see how the cows give milk?" Anthony asked.

Olivia sidled up against her mom. "I need to use the bathroom," she whispered.

As Angela waited for Mr. Moore's reaction, he let out a hearty laugh. "Nothing like having kids around. Come on in, everybody. David just phoned me this morning, so I didn't have a whole lot of time to straighten up."

The doorway led directly into the living room. There was a dark hardwood staircase with a landing, leading to the upstairs. It looked as if it had been trampled by many generations. The living room itself had plank flooring with gaps. A faded braided rug in shades of brown and red gave the room a homespun character, and curtains in an open-weave tan material hung on the two windows. A closed swinging door separated the living room from the space beyond. Noisy scratching sounded from behind the door.

"That's Blondie," the elder Moore explained, going toward the kitchen. "I didn't know if the kids were afraid of dogs or not."

"We like dogs," Michael told him, keeping step with him. "Can we play with her?"

"Sure you can. But she's big, and she thinks she's still a pup."

"How old is she?" Angela asked.

"Ten." When he opened the swinging door, the dog bounded into the living room and went straight to Angela, sniffing her hands, her purse and the hem of her jacket. Without hesitation, she crouched down and petted the dog, then scratched behind her ears.

"She likes you, Mom." Olivia was all smiles, too, then Angela remembered her request. Standing, she gave Blondie a last pat. "Can you tell us where your restroom is?"

"Sure," Aaron said, going into the kitchen. He pointed down a short hall. "Right there, next to the dining room."

The boys stayed in the living room with David and Blondie while Olivia went into the powder room and closed the door.

David's father turned to Angela. "So, are you and my son seeing each other?"

Suddenly David was beside her. "Don't give her the third-degree, Dad. We're not dating. I told you on the phone, I'm in a Big Brother program with Anthony."

Angela heard the strain in David's voice, saw Aaron Moore's back straighten and his eyebrows lift a little. There was tension there, and she had the feeling it wasn't just from the question he'd asked.

Unzipping her jacket, she tried to keep her eyes away from David's. "My son's going through a rough patch. David's already made a difference."

Aaron looked from one of them to the other.

Michael came running into the kitchen as Olivia emerged from the powder room. "Can we go see the chickens now?" he asked. "It's snowing."

"It wasn't supposed to snow until after midnight," David's dad commented, though Angela knew he was taking everything in. "But early snows like this could come to nothing. You folks staying for dinner? I've got ground meat we can make into hamburgers or meat loaf, lots of potatoes, some frozen vegetables. It won't be fancy."

"Do you do much cooking?" Angela asked.

"I do what I have to."

"I don't mind helping you. I have a recipe for meat loaf the kids like."

"Sounds good to me, but I didn't ask you here to cook."

"I like to cook."

"I've got ice cream for dessert," he offered, "not that you might want it on a cold night like this."

"The kids like ice cream anytime."

He grinned at her. "I like a woman who can be flexible."

A short while later, after the kids had chased the chickens and Aaron was giving them a tour of the milking barn, the wind picked up, blowing against the big doors, making them bang even as the long wooden bar held them shut.

David went to a side door and looked out. "I think we've got a blizzard."

Angela took her attention from the milking paraphernalia and napping cows and went to stand beside him. She could hardly see to the house. "Oh, my gosh. It's going to put down inches in no amount of time at all. Are we going to be able to get home?"

"Stay the night," Aaron invited. "It's the only safe thing to do."

"We can't impose like that."

The older man shrugged. "No imposition. I still have bedrolls in the attic. I'm sure the kids would like a campout."

Anthony, who had been quieter than the others and taking in everything about the farm, came over to her. "It would be neat to stay, Mom. We could see how Mr. Moore collects eggs and everything."

"Yeah. And they could even help me with the morning chores," Aaron added with a grin.

David turned away from the blizzardlike snow. "Do you have someplace you have to be tomorrow?"

"No. Not really. But I…"

"You and Olivia can have my sister's old room. Anthony, Michael and I can bunk in my room. On the other hand, the upstairs is cold. We could light a fire and all sleep around the fireplace in the living room."

"Around the fireplace!" the kids chorused.

"Maybe we can roast marshmallows," Michael interjected, as if nobody had ever thought of such a thing.

"Sorry, son, I don't have marshmallows. But I do have microwave popcorn."

"It's your decision," David told Angela.

She could imagine lying in a bedroll with David beside

her. That was the problem. She could imagine it all too easily. But what choice did she have? "It wouldn't be safe for us to leave tonight, would it?"

"Not if it keeps snowing like this."

She wondered how she was going to get through the night, acting as if David were nothing but a mentor to her son. But she would. She'd just sleep on one side of the room with Olivia, and he could sleep on the other with the boys.

To his dad she said, "We'll accept your hospitality for tonight. Thank you. But we definitely will help with the chores."

"You want to feed the chickens?" David asked with a smile.

"Whatever I have to do." And she meant it. Her kids were happier than she'd seen them in a while and had forgotten all about the fact their dad didn't care what they did, where they were and who they associated with. This weekend was going to be good for them. Maybe good for her, too.

As long as she stayed away from David.

Although David had tried to give Anthony most of his attention since they'd arrived at his dad's, his cleanup time in the kitchen with Angela had urged him to rethink his premise that a man could restrain his desire around a woman if he had enough self-control. Shutting his libido down had never been a problem in the past—even with Jessica, who'd been model perfect, a sex kitten in bed and aggressive enough to fortify any man's dreams. However, he'd found with Jessica that sex was just sex. Afterward he'd still felt that empty spot in his soul. After they'd gotten engaged he'd assumed he'd just forever feel that way, no matter what woman was in his life. He'd always been a loner, and letting anyone into the secret-club corners of his heart had never been easy.

After he was in that crushing accident, he'd understood the saying—a man comes into the world alone and dies alone. He'd almost died and hadn't had any breathtaking, wonderful spiritual feelings from it. He'd simply come away from the whole experience with a knowledge that there was a flicker inside of him that hadn't let him give up. That flicker connected him with something greater than he was, and he had to do life right this time around. It *wasn't* a dress rehearsal.

After Angela rinsed the last soapy dish, she propped it in the drainer for him to dry. She'd taken off her red crew neck sweater and rolled up her sleeves. A few splashes of water dotted the front of her white oxford blouse and caused the material to mold to her seductively. He had to focus on something other than the soft swells of her breasts. Her pretty face wasn't much better, and when his gaze dropped to her lips—

"Your dad said he refused a dishwasher as a present from you and your sister because he didn't want his electric bills to go up."

David gave himself a mental shake so her words sank in. "Yeah. We can't convince him that he's spending as much on dish detergent as he would on electricity."

Angela laughed, dried her hands on a towel and considered him seriously. "What's the issue between the two of you?"

From years of practice, he thought he and his dad had been doing pretty well. But Angela was no slacker when it came to perception, and she'd seen through their civil, polite dad-and-son routine.

He glanced over his shoulder toward the living room. "How would you like to take a walk? The snow has let up."

For a few moments she hesitated, and then, as if deciding a walk with him in the frigid air was safe enough, she nodded. "Walking off supper would be good."

"My dad liked what you did with that meat loaf. The apples with the crumb topping were even more of a hit. You really are good in the kitchen."

"Cooking's a hobby I enjoy. I entered some recipes in a dessert contest. It's a national contest, and I doubt if I'll even place, but it was fun to create."

"Your office manager's job is cut-and-dried, isn't it?"

"It sure is. That's why chocolate, flour, sugar and cream excite me."

He laughed this time, liking her sense of humor, her optimistic attitude, her I-can-handle-anything outlook. Yet he still didn't know how much of it was real. He had been fooled by Jessica, whose sexy, I-want-you smile and comments and questions about his life had been more manipulation than interest. Angela had lots of burdens—financial, physical, emotional. Was she looking for help with some of that?

Had she accepted his invitation to come to the farm today for her son's sake? Or for some other reason?

Jessica hadn't liked anything that would make her uncomfortable—an evening walk trudging in the snow would have done that. He'd see how Angela fared.

Laughter and an excited howl sailed into the kitchen from the living room.

"I didn't know a game of Yahtzee could be so much fun," she remarked, looking his way.

"I think they're enjoying Dad's stories about life on

the farm as much as they are the game. I'll let him know we're leaving."

Standing in the doorway, he must have caught his father's attention. He walked his fingers in a motion to the back door. The kids' chattering and Michael's turn shaking the Yahtzee dice told Angela they hadn't even noticed.

When they'd come inside after the tour of the barn, the kids had run their jackets upstairs. He'd hung his and Angela's with his dad's on the old wooden clothes tree in the corner of the kitchen.

Now as he handed her her jacket, she asked, "Do you and your dad have sign language?"

"Of sorts."

She didn't question him further as they zipped up, but her gaze met his. Her damnably blue eyes got to him big-time. They seemed to hold a wealth of everything—tenderness and love for her kids, worries about the future, the sensual curiosity he was crazy to even think about exploring with her.

The kitchen door opened onto a glassed-in porch. Floodlights from the barn outside sent shadows and dim light into the area. After he led her across it, they stepped outside.

"Oh!" Her exclamation seemed genuine and he wondered what had caused it.

Then as he stood there, soaking in everything with her, he knew. The sky was a mysterious black that might not have finished coating the world in white. The floodlight on the barn revealed what had already happened—the tall firs in the yard were flocked with snow. The fields seemed to stretch forever in white, blue and gray shadow and finally, black, where no light touched.

"This is…" Angela's breath hung in the air with her

words. "This is *so* peaceful. Listen. No sound. No sound at all."

"That's good?" he asked.

"It's like being in a church with no one else there. There's something I can just feel here that I can't feel in town." She glanced up at him shyly. "You must think I'm being ridiculous."

"No. I don't think that at all. Come on. Let's walk toward the barn. If you get cold, we can duck inside."

"Are we going to be able to get out in the morning?" she asked with some concern as they made footprints in the fluffy, white powder.

"Sure. The neighbor has a plow on the front of his truck. He plows Dad's lane. The township takes care of the main roads, and salt trucks will be out before first light."

He deeply inhaled the crisp, clean air. It held an elixir town air couldn't match. But they hadn't come outside for this walk just for the air. He might as well get into the conversation that he wasn't eager to have. He knew Angela would come back to it if he didn't. "You asked about me and my dad."

Stopping, she turned toward him.

"After my accident, I knew his dreams were shattered, as well as mine. He never missed one of my games. Even when I went to college, he drove there every weekend I was on the field. The look in his eyes when we got the news I was drafted into the NFL—" David shook his head "—I'll never forget that moment and how happy he was…how proud he was of me."

"Then overnight everything changed," she guessed. "Did he have trouble getting used to it?"

"As much trouble as I did, though he never talked

about it. I came home here for my outpatient recovery. There were lots of silent drives to the physical therapy facility in town."

"You couldn't talk to him?"

"I couldn't talk to him. I felt as if I'd let him down."

"The accident wasn't *your* fault."

"No, it wasn't. I realized that…slowly. I realized I had to make something of my life, in spite of what had happened. Once I could finally use my leg to drive, I took a long excursion. It was aimless, and I don't know exactly what I was looking for. But I found Rosewood. Something about the town told me it would be a good place to settle. When I discovered the high school needed a football coach, that clinched it. I worked at the local lumber yard while I coached and saved every penny I could. That's how I bought the store."

"So, your dad just never accepted the fact you couldn't play football again?"

"No, he accepted that. But he still wanted me to bank the big bucks. He thought he knew how I could do it—I should become a sports agent."

It was too cold to simply stand still and he motioned again toward the barn. They walked that way once more.

"You didn't want to be a sports agent?"

"It wasn't me. Even if I had become a popular NFL player like Duke, I would have handled it differently. I hated the limelight. I hated the cameras. I hated the interviews."

"Duke eats them up, doesn't he?" she said with a small smile.

"He sure does. He's good at all of it. But I'm much more private. I also didn't want to spend my life traveling from stadium to stadium."

"What about the income?"

"That's all my dad thought about. But I had to find something that was mine, that I could make a success, that would suit my personality. I love sports of all kinds. I knew about the equipment before I bought the store. And I love coaching football, too."

"But your dad envisioned more."

"I think he only knows what he's seen in the movies. Jerry McGuire, for example. I think he still holds hopes that I'll sell the store and try a new career—the one he chose for me. But it's not going to happen."

They reached the barn door. "Do you want to go inside?"

"No. I like it out here," she answered.

"But it's cold."

"I know. And as soon as my toes start going numb I'll let you know." They were standing in front of a holly bush. She playfully brushed some of the snow aside, revealing red berries. "You must have a male and a female or you wouldn't have the berries."

"I guess we must." Male and female. Even all bundled up as she was with her yellow knit ski cap, the turquoise and yellow jacket, her high black boots, she could be any man's winter fantasy. *The cold will keep your body in line,* he told himself as he took a step closer to her.

Gently he touched her cheek with his thumb. "Your cheeks are getting red."

She seemed to swallow hard, but then she asked, "You're not comfortable talking about your dad, are you?"

"No."

"It's easy to see he cares about you a lot. And you care about him."

"Sometimes caring isn't enough. We're on different wavelengths and we can't seem to find common signals."

"I know what that's like," she admitted. "Not being on the same wavelength with parents. After my parents divorced—it was my dad's fault because he had an affair and fell in love with someone at work—he just left, and my mom changed. The three of us had once been a happy family. Then they adopted my sister, Megan. For a few years Megan and I thought we had the happiest family on earth. But then everything came apart and Mom changed."

"How?"

"She'd always been somebody we could go to. Then suddenly, she simply wasn't there for us anymore. She was filled with so much anger at my dad that she didn't want him to see us. She didn't want us subjected to him and his—*floozy* was the word she used over and over. He gave up trying to make arrangements to visit. She was in her own world. She hadn't worked before the divorce. Afterward, she did. But she couldn't wait for Megan and me to find our own lives. All she wanted to do was leave Rosewood. I think every time she looked at us she thought about what her life had been. So we made her sad and angry and upset."

"What about now?" David asked. "Do you see her much?"

"No, we don't. She moved to South Carolina and has a circle of friends. She told me once she'd never remarry, and I believe her."

"Doesn't she want to see her grandkids?"

"I think grandkids make her feel old, and she doesn't want to feel old. We drive down there every summer and spend a week with her. Sometimes she visits in the spring or fall. But my kids don't enjoy being with her. She's removed from them like she was removed from us. And my dad…Megan and I don't hear from him except for Christmas cards. He and his wife are living in Arkansas this year. They move around a lot."

Angela and David stood in the cold, gazing at each other, understanding. The silence of snow-covered fields, the moonless sky and the world going to sleep on a winter night surrounded them. A slight breeze didn't have enough lift to ruffle the fringes of Angela's scarf, but she felt it along her cheek. She'd been about to tell David her feet were getting cold and they should probably go back. But now, looking into his eyes, seeing them darken with the same heated curling that had been twittering inside of her ever since she had met him, the words didn't come out. She didn't want to be anyplace but here with him.

She held the voices at bay that wanted to remind her she was being foolish. Nothing good could come of this. They had separate lives. She had a huge mortgage and kids and more responsibility than she'd ever imagined she could handle. That's what made her older than he was, not simply the three years.

Yet studying David's face, she not only found the small lines around his eyes that told her he'd weathered a few storms along with playing a sport he loved, but he'd had his life taken away from him, too, in a different way than she had when Jerome had left.

His voice was a husky baritone that seemed to fit perfectly into the hushed night. "I've told myself I should stay away from you."

Still trying to stave off a need she didn't understand, she reminded him, "I have a lot of baggage…besides three kids."

"I've got some of my own."

Without being a mind reader, she understood that he'd

loved and gotten hurt, too. "Then what are we doing? Dabbling in a little excitement?"

"A little?" he asked, a smile quirking up his lips. "I think we're dealing with more than a little."

Then he was surrounding her with his warmth, insulating her against the cold, lowering his lips to hers and filling her with so much anticipation she thought she'd burst. There was nothing forced about the kiss. It seemed so natural. She welcomed the tautness of his lips, the brush of his beard stubble against her cheek, all the highly intoxicating sensations, the tumbling into a world she'd never experienced. Oh, she'd kissed men before, but never like this. She'd never had this I-want-to-climb-into-you desire that made her breath come in shallow pants, that had her heart racing and her knees weakening. Neither of them could seem to get enough— not enough taste or tongues or breaths that were filled with each other.

After he broke away once, he came back again and everything about the kiss escalated. Their padded jackets interfered with pressing together. Their gloves inhibited touching. Wrapped in David's warmth, pictures ran through her head of what his naked body might look like—muscles, tanned skin, broad shoulders, slim hips…

She stopped there, got some sense and backed away.

He wouldn't let her back away far, though. "You started thinking," he accused her.

Actually, she hadn't. She'd been picturing, and she'd been *feeling* way too much.

"I realized something on the drive here today." Raising her chin, she finally looked at him.

"This isn't going to be good, is it?" he asked rhetorically.

"It isn't good or bad. I realized that when I married

Jerome, I wanted to be a mom more than I wanted to be a wife. Maybe I was the one who dropped the ball by not putting enough effort into making our marriage romantic. Maybe *I* was the reason intimacy never felt like more than coexisting. Maybe *I'm* the one who couldn't give enough, or receive, to make it work."

"You want to take on the whole burden of the failure of your marriage?"

"Of course not. But don't you see? Even if it didn't start out that way, my kids became so important that Jerome always came second. What man could ever want that?"

He peered into the distance as if he was sorting his words. Taking her cheeks between his palms, he said quietly, "You're more than a mom."

Her chest felt tight. "I'm not so sure about that most of the time. It goes back to that twenty-four-hour-a-day thing. The responsibility never goes away, David. Unless you have kids, you can't understand it."

"You're using them as an excuse." He dropped his hands from her. "You're afraid of this attraction between us, and you want to run from it."

"I have good reasons to run from it. Three of them. Not to mention how complicated you and I would make everything between you and Anthony."

"You can't stop living, dating and having sex because you have kids. You're a woman, too, Angela."

"I'm trying to be Super mom, remember? Super moms can put their needs aside. I have since Jerome left."

David's eyebrows went up and there was doubt in his eyes. That was the whole point of this, too. They didn't even *know* each other. If he *did* know her, he'd believe what she told him.

"How long has he been gone?"

"Three years."

"And you want me to believe…"

Now she really did pull back. Pulled out. Pulled away. "I don't care what you believe, David. It simply doesn't matter. I'd better go back in before one of the kids comes looking and we have a lot of explanations to give."

As she walked away from him, he called after her, "One easy explanation. We went for a walk."

She kept walking. The idea of having an affair with David was taunting, tempting and much too exciting. But she was Super mom. She didn't need sex *or* a man. Except for a few problems here and there, she was handling everything just fine.

Just fine.

David's digital watch told him it was almost 3:00 a.m. when he heard Anthony scoot out of his bedroll and quietly tiptoe through the kitchen to the bathroom. David had insisted Angela take the sofa. He was on his dad's oldest recliner, the one that went almost the whole way back. He'd shoved the coffee table aside, and the kids lay in a row in their bedding on the braided rug. He was acutely aware of Angela and their near argument or disagreement or whatever it had been.

Damn it, she was frustrating. The trouble was, he did understand where she was coming from. She'd worn a pair of his sister's old sweats to bed, but before she'd tucked herself into that sofa, he'd seen the curves underneath. He'd remembered the softness of her skin and the silkiness of her hair. Every time she turned over, he imagined her turning toward him in his bed.

He heard the water run in the bathroom and smiled. Earlier, Anthony had grumbled about how difficult it was to wash one hand with one hand. But he was doing it, which proved he listened to his mom, whether she thought he did or not. Instead of hearing the boy's footsteps continue in the kitchen, however, he heard the refrigerator open and the rattle of a dish.

One-handed was tough.

Going into the kitchen, David realized the aromas of supper still remained. With that meal Angela had endeared herself to his dad for life.

David had put on a pair of pajamas he'd left in his room for propriety's sake, even though he never wore them. They'd been left over from his stint in rehab. Anthony was wearing one of his old flannel shirts.

Standing before the refrigerator, the light shining on his bare feet, Anthony tried to angle the dish with the apple cobbler to the side of the shelf to get leverage.

"Hungry?" David asked.

The boy jumped, then kept his voice low. "I didn't know anybody else was awake."

Instead of asking Anthony if he needed help, David said, "I got awake and was hungry, too. Think there's enough left there for both of us?"

Anthony grinned. "We'd better leave some for Mr. Moore, or he'll be mad."

"I think he'd forgive us, but we can leave some. Want a glass of milk with it?"

Anthony nodded.

There was a counter at the far side of the kitchen, away from the living room, with high-backed wooden stools. David took the cobbler, milk, dishes and forks over there and sat beside the nine-year-old. "So, are you glad you came this weekend?"

Anthony's tough-guy attitude warred with what he really wanted to say. Finally, he admitted, "Yeah. I just wish…"

"What do you wish?"

"I just wish my dad would take us to his place some-times so we could camp out like this. It'd be cool."

"Where does your dad live?"

"He moved into a condo on the other side of Rosewood. He's got plenty of room. He even has two bedrooms."

"Your mom said your dad was starting up a new business. That could take a lot of time."

"Even before that, when he worked at the other place, he didn't ask us to come over. He'd take us to the movies, buy us popcorn, then drop us off. That was it. I don't think—"

David waited. But when he realized Anthony needed a bit of prompting, he asked, "What do you think?"

"I don't think he wants us around."

In spite of the urge to reassure Anthony, David didn't say that wasn't true, because he didn't know. He wouldn't lie to the boy. "I'll bet he misses you and will want to spend some time with you over the holidays." He was sure Angela would do everything in her power to make that happen, because she knew how important it was to the kids.

"You really think so?"

"I really think so." In the morning he'd talk to her about it. In the morning—

Nothing would change between them. Maybe that was for the best.

Chapter Six

"And then when Mr. Moore showed me how to milk the cow—and he helped because I couldn't do it with one hand—the milk sprayed all over his jacket!" Anthony told Angela this as David came up behind her on the porch.

All of the kids had stories to tell and had being doing it the whole drive home. The weekend had been a blast and a success as far as they were concerned.

Angela just felt…sad. Whenever she thought about her walk with David, that absolutely shoot-to-the-moon kiss, she almost wished she wasn't a mom…almost wished she could think of herself first…almost wished her life were different.

After she unlocked the door, the kids charged inside.

David brushed by her with a bag of goodies his dad had sent along—fresh eggs, turnips and sweet potatoes.

Noticing her mailbox on the porch was full, the lid not closing, Angela pulled Christmas cards, bills and flyers from the metal box and carried them inside. When she lay the stack on the étagère in the foyer, it toppled over and everything slid to the floor. The kids were in the living room taking off their coats, but David appeared from the kitchen and helped her pick up the mail.

One envelope in particular caught her eye. "I wonder if this is—" The correspondence had come from Rosewood Bank and Trust.

"A Christmas card from someone you haven't heard from in a while?" David asked conversationally, trying to cover the awkwardness between them.

"I wish. I filled out a loan application a month ago. I was supposed to hear anytime."

Placing the Christmas cards more securely on the étagère, she quickly opened the envelope. It only took a few seconds for the words on the official letter to sink in.

"They denied me the loan," she murmured. "I thought sure if I worked at Felice's Nieces, too, I could get approved." She'd been hoping the home equity line of credit would see her through the next few months until she found a renter. Now she wasn't sure what she was going to do, and that shook her. Uncertainty shook her a lot.

"Hey. You look a little pale. Are you okay?"

"No, I'm not okay." She lowered her voice so the kids wouldn't hear. "Bills are mounting up faster than I can pay them. Living expenses just keep going up. If Jerome would just send me a check when he's supposed to, I wouldn't be so worried. But I can't depend on him. I'm sure my loan application was rejected because of his debt. It's affected my credit rating."

"I don't know your situation with your ex-husband, or where this house fits in, but did you ever think about selling it and getting something smaller?"

"Sell the house? Live away from our friends? That's not something I want to consider. The kids have had enough disruption. I want to keep something stable."

David didn't appear impressed with her argument. "You should also have the luxury of sleeping at night. When you don't know if you can pay the bills—" He shook his head. "The kids would adapt, Angela."

At that moment she felt as if David Moore were an intruder. He'd stepped into their lives and turned hers topsy-turvy. Anthony had connected with him this weekend, and she was glad of that. She really was. Yet part of her was a bit miffed, too, that *she* hadn't been able to help her son...that she hadn't been able to handle this on her own.

The good time they'd had at Cloverleaf Farm, the attraction she felt for David, the memory of the desire he'd stirred up with his kiss bubbled up and spilled over. "I can solve my own problems, David. You're Anthony's mentor, not mine."

The awkwardness between them suddenly transformed into something colder, something that made them strangers again.

David's eyes lost their warmth, his stance became rigid, his face set. "You're right. I *am* Anthony's mentor, not yours. I should never have even made the suggestion. But maybe, Angela, you need someone to advise you and to give you perspective, just as much as Anthony does. I'll say goodbye to him and then be on my way. I'll give you a call later in the week to figure out what he and I might be able to do next weekend."

Then he handed her the stack of Christmas cards and bills he'd picked up from the floor.

When she took them, she was careful to keep her fingers from touching his. As he went into the living room, she gazed down at the letter again. The words hadn't changed. But something in her life had to.

That night David was trying to do end-of-the-year bookwork on his home computer. He wasn't doing so well at concentrating. It was almost nine o'clock when his phone rang. Glad for a distraction, he picked it up, thinking it might be Duke.

It wasn't.

"Are you still speaking to me?" Angela asked hesitantly.

He leaned back in his swivel chair. "That depends. What do you have to say?"

"I'm sorry for snapping this afternoon. We had a wonderful time at the farm and I didn't even thank you for that. I guess I'm just feeling...crowded."

When he was silent for a while, not sure where he wanted to take this, she stepped in. "Would you accept Christmas cookies as an apology?"

In spite of himself, he smiled. "Bribes do always work well," he confided teasingly.

"I didn't mean it as a bribe. It's more of a peace offering."

"It's the season," he said blandly. Then, letting her off the hook, he relented. "I understand frustration. And you're frustrated as hell. The thing is, we can deny the attraction between us all we want, but it's still going to be there."

"It's making my life more complicated. And we both know it's a dead end."

"Do we? You reacted so strongly to my suggestion you sell the house, I have to wonder if you're over your ex-husband."

"Not wanting to move has *nothing* to do with Jerome. I am *so* over him."

Her voice was filled with a certainty that almost had him believing her. "You don't wish you had your family back together?"

"In theory, maybe. But I don't want Jerome back. Believe me, David, I don't."

After he let her think about it a few moments, her tone became considering. "Wanting to keep the house is probably more connected to my pride. I want to show him I can give the kids the same advantages they would have had if the marriage had worked out. But now I'm wondering if I can."

"You're not two people, and you don't have a whole family anymore. That's the reality of it."

"Can you see *your* life this clearly?" she asked, not at all defensively.

"I think I can. But then again, my dad thinks I can't. So it's all a matter of perspective. When do you work this week?"

"Tuesday night, Thursday night and until two on Saturday."

"The kids will be with the babysitter on Saturday?"

"I'm hoping Megan can watch them."

"I'll work at the store Saturday morning. Why don't I come by about one and pick up Anthony. I'll take him to the movies or something."

She was quiet, and he suspected what she was thinking. "You'd rather not be there when I pick him up. Right?"

"That would probably be best."

Yes, it probably would. But he didn't like it, and she didn't sound as if she did, either. They ended the call then, David wishing her a good night. He knew his was going to be anything but restful.

Angela sat in the family room, staring into the flames in the fireplace. The raised, gray-and-white brick hearth kept sparks away from the spruce-green carpet.

Did you ever think about selling it?

David's words haunted her. Would she have to sell the house? *Should* she do that? She really loved this place. She'd chosen every detail. The family room was comfortable with its chair rail, spruce and off-white wallpaper, many-pillowed sofa in wine-and-spruce plaid. Even the two oversize chairs, one in plaid like the sofa and the second in off-white flowers, were comfy, and her kids often fell asleep in them. The maple armoire entertainment center held a twenty-six-inch TV. The stereo system was gone now. Jerome had taken that and the computer, but not much else.

On the other hand, she was hanging on to all of it. Three years ago, she'd wanted the adjustment to be easy for the kids, as easy as it could be, and she hadn't changed anything—except for making the space over the garage into an apartment for Megan. That had enabled her sister to sell her house and put all of her capital into Design Solutions, her graphic arts business.

But when Megan moved out, Angela knew she'd either have to accept her sister's offer of a loan or sell the house.

"You look like you're ready to cry." The melodic female voice startled Angela. But then Megan's face registered, and she got up to hug her. "How was your trip?"

"Successful. I got the account."

Since Megan had become involved with Greg Banning, she'd changed, definitely for the better. Always self-confident at work, now she was self-confident in her personal life, too. Tonight she was dressed in a hot-pink sweater and slacks set. The monochrome look slimmed her full figure.

"You don't look as if you're going to settle down with a good book tonight or rest from your trip."

"I'm not. Even though we talked about five times a day, I missed Greg so much, I could scream. He's on his way over, but I wanted to check in with you and see how everything was going."

"If Greg's going to be here soon—"

"It'll take him at least half an hour. He's going to shower and change, and then pick up some takeout for us."

"Chinese in bed?" Angela teased.

"Probably." She took Angela's hand and tugged her down on the sofa. "So tell me why you look so unhappy."

Angela had been thirteen and Megan eleven when the Schumachers had adopted her, and they'd bonded from the first moment they'd set eyes on each other. Three years later when their parents divorced, they'd supported each other, cried together and tried to make sense of what had happened. They were still best friends, and Angela knew that would never change.

"Things have gotten…interesting while you've been gone."

Megan pulled one knee up onto the sofa and faced her. "Tell me."

Angela did, beginning with Anthony and ending with David, but not *everything* that had happened between her and David. She already felt foolish and still stunned that her attraction to him seemed so overwhelming.

"So…Anthony's warming up to this David Moore and you think the stories Rebecca heard weren't on the mark."

"I checked out what David told me, even calling the chief of police."

"And you went to his dad's farm?" Megan's eyebrows raised.

"Yes. Actually, it was a great experience for the kids. I'm sure they'll tell you all about it."

"What aren't *you* telling me?"

"Meggie—" She hadn't used that nickname for her sister since they were kids.

"Uh-oh. You're in trouble."

"I hope not," she declared vehemently. "He kissed me a couple of times. The earth moved. The stars burst. I got hot. But that happens to women every day of the week, doesn't it?"

Megan was staring at her as if she'd just developed a second head. "I'm not sure it's all that common, though it did happen to me and Zooey. And to Rebecca. And Carly. And Molly."

Five women on Danbury Way had found true love. "How do you know they all felt the earth move?"

"Because they've all told me at one point or another. I get around, sis. I don't have kids."

That brought a wry smile to Angela's lips. Then it slipped away. "He's younger than I am."

"As long as he's over eighteen that doesn't have anything to do with sex."

Angela swatted Megan's arm. "Get real!"

"How much younger?"

"Three years."

"Doesn't mean a thing."

"You know most men would run screaming from three kids, let alone a woman who has to take care of them. A woman who *likes* taking care of them."

"Has he run away yet?"

"It's been less than two weeks!"

"But it sounds like a lot happened in that time. And if Anthony's bonding with him—"

"Don't you see? That's the biggest part of this problem. Well, one of the biggest parts of this problem. Anthony's not going to want to share David, besides the fact that he'd think I'm turning my back on Jerome if I even look at anyone else."

"You don't know all this for sure. You haven't dated since your divorce."

"I know my son. I also know Jerome's lack of attention is bothering him greatly. If it seems like I'm taking David's attention from him, or his caring, or anything, he's going to be even more upset."

"Kids adjust."

"I'm not sure it's as easy as anyone thinks. Think about how we felt when *our* parents divorced."

Megan was frowning, now, too. "The thing is, Ange, in the long run, if you and this David Moore hooked up, wouldn't that be the best thing for the kids?"

"What man is going to be willing to take on the responsibility I've got? He even suggested I sell the house!" That had come out and she hadn't intended to explore that avenue right now.

Her sister's green eyes grew huge. "Is that something you want to consider?"

"No, it's not. But the bank denied my loan application and—"

"Why would you apply for a loan from the bank when you can have one from me interest free? Put your independence aside so you can sleep at night."

"I was thinking about that when you came in. The thing is—I don't know how long it's going to take me to pay you back."

"You don't have to worry about that. Greg is rich. My business is doing great. Money is *not* one of my concerns. So don't let it be one of yours."

"We have to put something in writing and work out a payment schedule."

"Angela…"

"I mean it, Meg. That's the only way I'll agree to it."

"Okay. Fine. The lawyer I use for Design Solutions can draw up something."

"I can start paying you bigger chunks once I get a renter for the garage apartment."

The front doorbell rang and Angela knew that would be Greg.

"I told him I'd be here."

"Do you want me to answer it, or do you want to do it?" Angela joked.

Megan was already on her feet. "I'll get it. But one last thing, sis."

"Dare I ask what?"

"You've got to follow your heart. I know you think the kids come first, but you've got to look at the *big* picture."

As Megan went to the door in the foyer, Angela sank back into the cushions on the sofa. Follow her heart. It had better give her darn good directions because she hadn't listened to it in a long time, and she didn't know if she'd even recognize its voice.

When Angela got home from work Wednesday evening, she was met by Megan and Olivia. The two of them were actually giggling.

"What's up?" she asked warily, as she took off her coat and hung it in the foyer closet.

"You have a date," Olivia informed her. "With Coach Moore," she added.

"I what?"

Anthony came thumping down the stairs. "You're not going to have dinner with him, are you, Mom?"

Feeling as if she'd just stepped into the middle of a typhoon, Angela looked to her sister for more explanation.

But Megan wasn't the one who gave it. Her daughter did. "I thought it would be nice if you and Coach Moore had dinner together. We called him and he's coming at six."

Angela glanced at her watch and saw that it was five-fifteen. "Tell me you're kidding."

"Aunt Megan says we have to go over to her apartment with her," Anthony grumbled.

Finally Megan intervened. "Anthony, you know I told you it would be nice for your mom to have dinner with an adult for a change. She needs company, too. Now gather up whatever you want to do and bring it along."

Motioning to the living room, Megan said, "I set up a table in there. I ordered coq au vin from that little French restaurant over on Poplar Street and I picked it up on my way home from work. It's heating in a casserole in the oven. Olivia helped me make a salad. There's a loaf of French bread, and—"

"Chocolate-raspberry cheesecake," Olivia added. "If there's any left over, Aunt Megan says we can have some."

"Go get Michael," Megan said to Anthony. "Put on your shoes and grab your coats. Come on. Let's scoot." She gave Angela's camel slacks and off-white sweater a once-over, then leaned close and whispered, "You can do better than that outfit. Go put on something sexy."

Angela backed away from her sister. "Are you out of your mind?"

Again, Megan leaned close. "This was Olivia's idea. Don't make her feel bad about it. Enjoy the dinner and whatever comes of it."

Five minutes later Megan and the kids had left and Angela was standing in her bedroom, peering into her walk-in closet. She had forty minutes.

To do what?

The fact that she had a date soon hit her hard. Stripping her clothes off as she went, she hurried to the shower, speed-soaped, washed her hair, then toweled off, trying not to think about what came next. If she thought, she'd probably have a nervous breakdown.

Thank goodness when she dried her hair, it cooperated. With a few strokes of her curling iron, at least her head was ready.

Sorting through her closet, she was at a loss. She hadn't gone on a date in years. Something sexy, Megan had said. It was almost Christmas, right?

She found a red dress that could be dressed up or down, depending on the occasion. When she slipped it on, she was relieved to see it still fit. She remembered wearing it for a business dinner with Jerome years ago. After adding a pair of black pumps that made her feel taller than a midget, she chose a casually elegant gold chain Megan had given to her last Christmas. She decided earrings would be overdoing it, added a brush of mascara to her lashes, a coat of lipstick to her lips and hurried downstairs to explore everything Megan had told her about in the kitchen. She actually felt dizzy thinking about David coming over. Megan hadn't told her what she'd said to him to get him to come.

Nervous all over again, Angela called her. When Megan picked up, Angela could hear the kids talking in the background. "What did you tell him?" Angela asked.

"That was easy. I just told him you wanted him to come for dinner to thank him for all the time he's given Anthony. Simple. Right?"

"Didn't he question why *you* were calling him instead of me?"

"Not exactly. I told him Olivia had made the suggestion and you were tied up at work, so I was the messenger."

Angela almost groaned. How could a man say no to that? Even if he was coming, she didn't know if he *wanted* to come.

The doorbell sounded. "I could wring your neck," she said to Megan.

Her sister laughed and hung up.

When Angela opened the door to David, she simply didn't know what to say to him. He was standing there in a navy crew neck sweater and khaki slacks, a bouquet of flowers in one hand, a bottle of wine in the other.

"Do I have the right house?" he joked.

Unmindful of dating protocol, she just knew she had to right this situation. She stepped back so that he could come inside, not taking the flowers or the wine from him. Instead she said, "I know you were probably coerced into this…this…date. So if you don't want to be here, I'll understand."

His gaze roved over her freshly washed hair, the gold chain at her neck, her high heels and everything else in between. Then he set the wine and the flowers on the étagère, stepping closer to her. "I accepted the invitation not knowing if *you* wanted me here."

His lime-scented aftershave teased her nose. She couldn't seem to get enough of him, staring at his angular face, the way his shoulders filled out the sweater, his slim hips. That tummy-twirling feeling was back, and it was almost hard to breathe. "I don't know if you *should* be here, but I want you here."

At her admission, he smiled and came even closer. Then, taking her chin in his hands, he lifted her lips to his. "I dreaned about you at night," he murmured, right before he set his lips on hers.

She didn't need a barometer to tell her a storm was on the way. She didn't need a thermometer to show her the temperature in the room had gone up at least ten degrees. She didn't heed the small voice in her head that was practically screaming, *This is a bad idea.*

His kiss *had* to be right when it felt so good. It took her out of herself, proved she wasn't just a Super mom, reminded her she was a woman. His tongue was demanding this time, expecting a response, and she gave it to him.

Suddenly he broke away. Breathing hard, he looked down at her. "We'd better slow down if we want to get through dinner."

Laughing self-consciously, she took a deep breath. "Dinner's in the oven. You can make yourself comfortable in the living room."

"Or I could help you get it out."

Jerome had never helped her in the kitchen. Never helped her anywhere, really. "I might drop something if you get too close. My hands are still shaking from that kiss," she kidded him. Yet she knew it was true.

He slid his hand under the hair at the back of her neck and massaged a little. "Relax, Angela. I'm not going to jump your bones. We're going to have dinner."

"Maybe I was thinking about jumping *your* bones," she admitted.

Now he laughed. "I really like an honest woman." Then a shadow crossed his face, and she wondered where it had come from and what had caused it.

Dropping his hand, he motioned toward the kitchen. "I promise I won't get too close. We'll deal with temptation after we eat."

They were silent as they carried dinner into the living room. Megan had even started a fire, though Angela didn't need flames to keep her warm. Not the kind that came from wood, anyway. Just looking at David did that. Just seeing those gold flecks in his hazel eyes that told her he was remembering the kiss as much as she was…that they were both thinking about what came next. It seemed as if she had known him longer than she had, and she didn't understand why that was so.

Megan had set a globed candle on the table. David lit it with the matches that were lying beside it.

Once they were seated across from each other, the fire, the candlelight and the Christmas tree lights casting intimate shadows, the low lighting in the room adding to the datelike feel of their dinner, Angela confided, "I haven't dated in years."

"Isn't it like riding a bicycle?" Amusement danced in his eyes.

"Not these days. I have so many questions, but I'm not even sure if I should ask them."

"You won't know unless you do." He was serious now, and she realized if he didn't want to answer a question, he'd tell her so. Unlike Jerome, David was a communicator.

"All right. Are you dating right now? I mean, anyone else?"

"No. I haven't in a long time. There hasn't been anyone I *wanted* to date."

She suspected there had to be a reason for that. "Have you ever dated anyone seriously?"

"Yes, I have."

"But it didn't end well? And that's why you haven't dated?" she prodded.

The phone rang, forestalling his answer if he was about to give one.

"I'll let the machine get it." She nodded to the answering machine sitting by the phone on the end table.

The phone rang the requisite four times. David

concentrated on the food on his plate, and she knew their conversation wasn't going to resume until the distraction passed. If this was Megan or Olivia trying to find out how the date was going—

"I'm trying to reach Angela Schumacher," the male voice said. "Ms. Schumacher, this is Thomas Brolin, from Sweeney and Company test kitchens. Our company sponsored the Great Christmas Dessert Contest."

Angela's gaze met David's, and he murmured, "You'd better take it."

Hopping up from her chair, she went to the end of the sofa and snatched up the phone. "Mr. Brolin, this is Angela Schumacher." Aware of David watching her, she took a deep breath and waited.

"Ms. Schumacher, we have what I hope is exciting news for you. You were one of four finalists whose recipes will be considered for the winner of our contest. But we will need you in our test kitchen in Poughkeepsie on Friday at 10:00 a.m. Can you be there?"

Realizing she'd have to ask for the day off, she hesitated.

"Ms. Schumacher?"

"I'll be there," she decided, not knowing where this was going to lead, but ready for new possibilities in her life.

"Terrific. We'll have all the ingredients you need, the baking pans you prescribed. You just need to bring yourself and your talent. And if your deluxe Christmas torte is the best recipe, you'll be making it on *The Breakfast Show* next week. Do you have an e-mail address where I can send you specifics?"

She didn't own a computer, since Jerome had taken the

family one, so she rattled off Megan's e-mail address. After Mr. Brolin gave her a contact number, she hung up the phone, dazzled, amazed and feeling incredibly lucky.

"Good news?" David asked.

"I'm a finalist!" burst from her lips in a triumphant cry. "Can you imagine? Out of the whole country, I'm one of four people who gets to make their recipe for the judges."

David stood and came to her, obviously happy for her. "Nothing like this has ever happened before?"

"Not ever. And I've entered a lot of contests, just for fun. Oh, David. What if I win? I'll be on *The Breakfast Show.*"

Laughing, he took her in his arms, lifted her off the ground and swung her back to her feet. They gazed into each other's eyes and the magic began all over. The pull. The longing. The hunger. And the need. Maybe it was just plain lust. Maybe she just needed someone to hold her and touch her and kiss her. But when David wrapped his arms around her, thrills shot through her. When his lips came down on hers, she could hardly remember her name.

"No!" Anthony's voice shot through her like a tearing lance. It wasn't in her head, was it?

Breaking away, she saw her son's red face, his wind-blown hair, his horrified expression. Pulling herself out of David's arms, she moved toward him, but he turned and ran.

"Anthony, wait," she and David called at the same time.

But her nine-year-old ran into the kitchen, and she heard the back door slam. She froze, considering what she was going to say when she caught up with him. She didn't have a clue about how she was going to clean up this mess.

Chapter Seven

David called Anthony's name, racing after him. He knew this was the worst possible scenario that could have happened.

Or maybe the best.

If he and Anthony talked this out, if he and Angela sat her son down, they could make him understand that his mom needed friends, too.

Actually his mom needed more than friends. David had tried putting aside his attraction to her, but it was a no-go. Tonight, when she'd opened her door to him, he'd realized why. Their growing bond was more than physical. He liked the woman. He respected her. She was struggling to do what was best for her and her family and *wasn't* looking for a rescuer. He was almost sure of that now. She just kept putting one foot in front of the other, hoping her next step would be the best one for everyone.

Through the kitchen and into the breezeway, David called Anthony's name again. He zoomed by the natural wicker furniture into the garage and there he saw the boy go out the door through the back.

He caught up with him at the foot of the stairs leading to Megan's apartment. She'd come out, but David waved her off.

Angela's sister stayed where she was but didn't go inside. He clasped Anthony's arm. "Wait a minute. We have to talk."

"I don't wanna talk to you," Anthony mumbled and pulled away.

"Your mom and I are getting to know each other. We like each other."

"Go away," Anthony shouted and ran up the stairs.

By now, Angela had arrived, too, and as Anthony raced into Megan's apartment, she put a restraining hand on David's shoulder. "He's not going to listen to you. It's better if I talk to him."

"We should *both* talk to him."

"No, David. This is *my* doing. It's my fault. I knew this kind of thing could happen. I'll try to smooth things over, but I don't know if that's going to be possible."

"If you'd just let me speak with him…" David suggested.

"And what are you going to say? That we like kissing each other? He's nine!" She let out a huge sigh. "I want to salvage his relationship with you if I can. And I definitely don't want him to think I was trying to steal you away. This is *so* complicated."

The whole idea of Angela talking to Anthony alone didn't sit well with David. He was part of this. If he was part of the problem, he should be involved in the solution. But he had no rights where Angela and her kids were concerned. If they did start dating seriously, would she let him in? Would she let him break into this family that had had to survive on its own for three years?

Running his hand through his hair, he gazed up at Megan's closed door. "I don't want you to shut *us* down. I don't want you to let Anthony think he can control your life. Don't give him that kind of power, or he'll become even more of a tyrant."

"He has to know he's loved."

"Yes, he does. But *loved,* not entitled to get whatever he wants just because his dad won't pay attention to him. This is the problem you had in the first place, Angela."

Although she worried her lower lip as if she were thinking about his words, she didn't relent. "I know what you mean. But I've got to take care of this with him myself. It's probably better if you stay away for a while."

He didn't like that idea at all. "That's no solution."

"It is for now." She put her hand on his arm. "Please, David, just let me handle this. Okay?"

Her blue eyes were beseeching, and he knew she was trying to do what was best. He didn't think what was best was not seeing her again, and he had a feeling this was where her reasoning was headed. "If you push me out of your life, you won't solve anything with Anthony."

"Just give me some time," she said in a low voice that he thought shook a little.

Maybe this was hard for her, too. Maybe her feelings for him were more than simple attraction. If they weren't, he probably wasn't going to see her after tonight. She *would* put Anthony first, whether that was best for everybody or not.

"Call me if you need my help," he told her.

Their gazes held for a few long moments, and hers became shiny with emotion. But then she turned and ran up the stairs, a Super mom once more, ready to put her son before everything else in her life.

David now understood what Angela had meant when she'd told him a man would always come second.

Was there any point in pursuing her when she was always going to be ready to put her life on hold for her kids?

On Thursday morning, Anthony still wasn't talking to her about seeing her kissing David last night…about school…about anything. He wasn't talking to Olivia or Michael, either. Finally Angela decided to give it all a rest. "Finish breakfast. Five minutes and that school bus will be here."

Detouring through the living room to the kitchen for a few minutes to catch the weather, she switched on the TV with the remote. As she caught the tail end of the weather, she couldn't help thinking about David… thinking about what could happen between them if they'd both give it a chance. She'd tried to explain to Anthony that David would still be his friend, even if she and the coach saw each other on a social basis. But sullen and silent, Anthony had seemed to turn off her words.

Sun was forecasted for the next few days. At least she wouldn't have to worry about the weather tomorrow when she traveled to the test kitchen.

She was about to click off the TV with the remote when the local anchor appeared with breaking news. "At this gift-giving time of the year," a tall brunette with a pretty smile said, "apparently someone decided to steal a few gifts of his own. Moore's Sporting Goods was broken into sometime last night. Mr. Moore has declined an interview, but our police chief will give a few comments when he's finished inside."

As Angela studied the screen, she saw the area around David's store was a three-ring circus. She wanted to call him but felt awkward because she hadn't made any progress with Anthony. In spite of her best intentions, absolute sadness overtook her when she thought about not seeing him again. She had to ask herself, what good would that do? Would Anthony suddenly start talking to her? Would he become a happy child again? He and David had been getting closer, and it was a friendship that Anthony needed.

Suddenly making up her mind, she decided to stop at Moore's Sporting Goods on the way to work.

Twenty minutes later, only one police car remained out front. Angela noticed powder residue on the door and wondered if she could get inside. Peering through the glass, she spotted David walking toward her. That heart-thumping awareness began.

When he opened the door from the inside, he was obviously surprised to see her there. "Angela!"

"Hi. I heard about the robbery on the news."

"You're here because of the robbery?"

She wasn't sure, but she thought she saw a flicker of disappointment in his eyes. Had he thought she'd come because everything was resolved with Anthony?

"I was worried. The reporter didn't say anyone was hurt, but with a burglary, you never know."

His expression lost some of its tension and gentled. "You thought I got hit over the head?"

"I didn't know. I also didn't know if you'd…call."

Taking her by the arm, he led her inside, away from the curious looks of people going by who wanted to know what had happened. After he guided her as far as a shelf with fishing gear, he stopped. "I was going to call you tonight to wish you luck for tomorrow."

He hadn't forgotten about her chance to win fifteen minutes of fame. "I'm going to need it."

"What you're going to need is all your attention focused on that dessert. What's happening with Anthony?"

"He's shutting me out. No big surprise there. He won't listen. I know he thinks I betrayed him, and maybe I did."

"You did nothing of the sort. I still think I need to talk to him."

"No, David. Not yet. Let's just let everything…cool down."

Taking her hand, he brought it to his lips and kissed her fingertips. Tremors rippled through her body.

"Things aren't going to cool down just because we don't see each other," he warned her.

"If you only knew how torn I feel about this."

"We should confront the situation head-on."

"I just don't think that will work. I'm afraid it will put an even wider gap between me and my son. Please try to understand that."

He obviously didn't, and there was nothing she could do about that. Not right now. "Tell me what happened here."

If they focused on something else, maybe she wouldn't notice the scent of his aftershave. Maybe she wouldn't want to slip her hand under his pullover sweater and feel those muscles across his shoulders. Maybe she wouldn't want him to kiss her and kiss her and kiss her until darkness fell and no one existed but the two of them.

Soberly he explained, "Someone must have hidden in the storeroom closet until the store closed."

Although David's statement had been matter-of-fact, something about his tone made her ask, "Do you know who?"

"Not for sure. But I have a suspicion. Between coaching and mentoring, I meet a lot of kids. There was a boy last year I had to cut from the team for being late for practices. Afterward he told me he'd get me back for cutting him. Coincidentally, he's been in and out of the store a couple of times the past few weeks."

"Did you tell the police?"

"I don't have any proof. I can't accuse him of anything when all he did was come in and look around. If I'm right about this, it's something I should handle myself."

"No." The word erupted from her, hard and fast.

This time David put both hands at her waist and brought her closer. "You *do* care."

Care? She was afraid she more than cared, and that was absolutely ridiculous. She couldn't have fallen for a man this fast. Yet when she looked into David's eyes, all her worries seemed to lift. She got aroused as she'd never been aroused before, and she wanted to spend time alone with him. Alone. When there were three kids in the wings, and one who didn't want to have anything to do with either of them right now, how would *that* ever happen?

She wouldn't let David kiss her. She wouldn't. She'd fall apart at his feet if he did that, and she couldn't handle wobbly knees the rest of the day.

Backing out of his embrace, she glanced at her watch. "I have to get to work or I'll be late."

When he frowned, there was frustration written all over him. "You're shutting me out."

"No, I'm just…retreating a little."

After a long, steady look, he asked, "Will you let me know how tomorrow goes?"

"I have no idea what time I'll be back, and I'm taking the kids to the community center tomorrow night. We're helping to put together holiday baskets."

"I'll be there, too. I'm going to be delivering them."

She might have suspected as much. "If Anthony's along, we might not get a chance to talk."

"If Anthony's along, you're going to have to show him that he doesn't run your life."

"Oh, David."

"Don't tell me I don't understand…because I do. Just remember, *you're* the parent. He's the kid. He takes his cues from you." Snatching her hand and tugging her toward him, he gave her a hard, deep, quick kiss.

Afterward, Angela drew away, then left his store. Her knees were definitely going to be wobbling the rest of the day.

She was just going to have to deal with it.

The test kitchen was every cook's dream. Even with three women and one man using it, they didn't bump into each other often, because of the many sinks, stove-tops and multiple ovens. Stainless steel gleamed from corner to cabinet, from refrigerator to granite counter. Angela simply loved kitchens. She felt useful in them and, for the most part, in control and totally immersed in whatever she did. Today she tried to forget she was in the running for the prize—a cooking spot on *The Breakfast Show*. She told herself she was making her chocolate rum torte simply for company—Megan, Greg and her neighbors.

David, too? a curious little voice asked.

She was trying not to think of David today, just as she was trying not to think of the judges who would decide if her torte was the best dessert.

As she kept an eagle eye on her chocolate melting in a double boiler, a woman dressed in jeans with little candy canes embroidered on them and a red-and-white-striped shirt heard a beep coming from her pocket. Taking a little silver phone from there, Linda Zahn stopped grating the carrots that were one of the ingredients in her pineapple carrot cake with cream cheese icing. As soon as Angela had heard about the recipe, she knew this woman would be giving her a run for that TV spot. She seemed to be about Angela's age, maybe younger. It was hard to tell. But she wore her wavy, black hair tied back in a ponytail and was constantly pushing her rimless glasses higher on her nose.

One of the other contestants was running a mixer, so Angela didn't hear any of Linda's conversation. Yet, when she took the chocolate off the burner to cool and saw her close her phone, she realized the woman was crying. Linda searched in her pocket for a tissue and came up empty.

Grabbing one from her own pocket, Angela handed it to her. "Are you okay?"

The mixer suddenly stopped, and Christmas carols piped in on an overhead speaker camouflaged their voices. "I've never been away from my husband before. We've been married three years. We just had a baby six months ago and I miss them both so much."

"Where do you live?" Angela asked.

"Ohio. I flew in yesterday and stayed in a hotel last night."

Angela didn't know if she was stepping into a mine-field asking questions, but she did anyway. "Do you wish you hadn't come?"

"Oh, no. We knew this would be a big adventure for me. Both of us couldn't afford to come, and I just didn't want to travel with the baby. I was a little worried about John taking care of her, but he says he's doing okay."

"You trust him with her?"

"Oh, yes. He's helped me since the day she was born. We alternate getting up at night. He's taking vacation days today and tomorrow."

What Linda had told Angela astonished her. "You take turns getting up with the baby?" She simply had never known a man on earth who had done that.

"She was colicky the first couple of months, so we didn't get much sleep. But you know, I think we bonded even more completely then, walking her back and forth, taking turns, making hot chocolate so we could stay awake if we had to. This Christmas is going to be so special. Do you have children?"

"I have three. Five, seven and nine." Angela was still turning over everything Linda had told her. "And you really trust your husband with the baby?"

"Don't you trust your husband?"

"I'm divorced."

Looking as if she'd just made the biggest faux pas of

her whole life, Linda apologized. "Oh, I'm so sorry. I shouldn't have assumed. You aren't wearing a wedding ring, but I just thought you'd taken it off for cooking."

"No, I've been a single mom for three years." She smiled and covered the awkward moment by saying, "If you'll excuse me, I have to make sure my chocolate is the right temperature."

"Of course. Maybe we can talk a bit after we're finished. I feel so alone here. Do you know what I mean?"

Actually, Angela didn't. She'd never had the kind of connection this woman obviously had with her husband. What would it be like to actually find a soul mate? "Sure, we can talk. I took the day off, so maybe we can find somewhere to have lunch, if you'd like."

"I'd like that a lot."

As Linda went to the sink to wash her hands, Angela moved back to her pot of chocolate. If she didn't *expect* to find a soul mate, how would she ever find one? If she didn't take the risk of trusting a man again, how would she ever know if she *could* trust one?

David's ruggedly handsome face popped in front of her eyes. She could almost hear his deep voice, see the warmth on his face when he talked about Anthony, feel the heat that emanated from him whenever he came close to her. She thought about her kids and how they'd taken to him. Even Anthony, before he'd caught them kissing. After spending a few visits with David, he'd almost been the boy she once knew. He'd been smiling again. At Cloverleaf Farm, he'd been a happy and carefree nine-year-old. David had done that for him. David had supported Anthony through the whole broken-arm episode and bonded with him in a way she'd never seen Anthony bond with a man. Certainly not Jerome. Anthony had just tagged along after him, and his dad had not respected him for the child he was.

Whenever Angela was in the same room with David, she felt drawn toward him. Pure, physical attraction seemed to exert the magnetic pull. Yet something else was there, too. Something less tangible. Something almost… mystical?

She was losing it, that was for sure. There was nothing mystical about David's kisses or how she felt when she was in his arms.

Yet her heart felt touched after he kissed her, not just her lips.

Should she give them a chance? Should they try to work things out with Anthony as a couple?

David was going to be on her mind today. So be it. She'd imagine she was making this Christmas torte just for him.

The community center's game room was buzzing with activity. The pool table had been pushed against the wall under the antidrug poster, and the air hockey game sat against a side wall under a string of art projects kids had made. The volunteers had taken over the whole place tonight. Baskets and boxes were spread from one corner to the other along with food donations.

Angela handed Michael a can of stewed tomatoes. "In that basket," she pointed to one to the left of him.

Olivia and Anthony were helping Carly and Bo on the other side of the room. Already Angela's trip to the test kitchen this morning seemed like a dream. She was back into her daily routine, and Anthony was still withdrawing from her. On top of that, she hadn't been able to reach Jerome to talk to him about spending time with the kids over the holidays. If she didn't reach him soon, she was going to go camp out on his doorstep until he got home so they could have a face-to-face conversation.

Stooping over to help Michael fill his basket, Angela was startled when she felt a hand on her shoulder.

Megan smiled. "Why don't you let Michael help me and Greg for a while?"

Angela caught the sight of Greg, who was already lining up boxes on the floor. "You suddenly crave the company of a five-year-old?"

With a wrinkle of her nose, Megan leaned close to Angela. "You filled boxes. They should go to the storeroom now. Someone's in there loading up his SUV so he can deliver them."

"Someone?"

"Yes, someone, with a capital *D*."

Lifting a filled basket, Megan handed it to her sister. "Here, take it in." She caught Michael's hand. "Come on, Michael. We're going to help Greg."

Angela stood there a few moments, holding the basket, debating with herself what she should do. Seeing that Anthony and Olivia were occupied as well as Michael, she hurried to the storeroom with the basket.

The storeroom was empty. Well, it was filled with food, but David wasn't there.

Setting her basket in a grouping of five others, she was about to return to the game room when the outside door opened and shut. There he was—tall, blond and handsome, his down jacket making his shoulders look even broader, his jeans fitting his powerful legs way too well, his sudden smile already causing goose bumps on her arms.

"I was going to come looking for you as soon as I got the rest of these loaded."

"You were?" After her quick departure from his store yesterday, she was surprised he still wanted anything to do with her. He came near her but didn't touch her. Oh, how she wanted him to touch her.

"Did your torte turn out well?"

"I think so. I hope so. I hope it tasted as good as it looked."

"When will you find out if you won?"

"It's possible I'll get a call tonight or tomorrow." She pointed to her jeans pocket. "I have my cell phone on vibrate, as well as ring. How about you? Anything new on the burglary?"

She knew she was stalling for time, making conversation. But she needed to shore up her courage for what she wanted to say to him.

"I went to see the boy I told you about."

One thing she already knew about David—he was proactive. When he saw something that needed to be done, he didn't hesitate to do it. "How did that go? Could you tell if he was involved?"

"Conner wouldn't admit anything. But he wouldn't meet my eyes directly. He fidgeted the whole time, and I think he knows *I* know that he did it. In a roundabout way, I told him that stealing won't take care of his problems, whatever they are—whether it's settling a grudge with me or providing for his family for Christmas."

Although Angela still thought of David as a younger

man, she realized his experiences had given him wisdom. "Do you think this Conner stole because his family needed things?"

"His dad was let go from his job and hasn't worked for a year, and his mom has some health problems. She's been working on and off. He has two younger sisters."

"Is the family on our list?" She motioned to the baskets still sitting there.

"No, they're not. They're a proud family. My guess is they didn't sign up."

"Do you think they'd accept one if they got it anyway?"

"I don't think they'll turn Santa away."

"Good. Then let's put a basket together for them and you can deliver it."

He hadn't touched her up until that point. He hadn't moved any closer. But now he did. When he ran his thumb over her cheek and then across the point of her chin, she tried to keep the melting-at-his-feet reaction from her face.

She must have done a good job because he asked, "Are you going to keep running from me?"

"Don't *you* want to run? It's not just me, David. I come with Olivia and Michael, and most of all, Anthony."

"I've never run from anything, and I won't start now. I think we should go for pizza tomorrow night. *All* of us. I want to have a talk with Anthony first. If we can't come to some understanding and he wants to sit by himself and not associate with us, he can do that. But he'll learn to get used to us being together. On the other hand, I'm not going to force myself on him or on you. What do *you* want?"

This afternoon she'd realized exactly what she wanted. "I don't know if I'm rationalizing or not, but I can't let Anthony run my life. Or take something away from his brother and sister that they need, too. I have to take all their feelings into consideration. We have to work through this with them, and Anthony has to see he's part of a family, not just a little bully who gets his way when he acts out."

"This wasn't an easy decision for you to make," David said, obviously seeing that it wasn't.

"I'm trying to do what's best for everyone, and…and I don't want to stop seeing you."

Smiling now, he glanced over his shoulder as they heard voices coming closer to the storage room. "I'd kiss you if I could, but I think that's going to have to wait until tomorrow night when the kids are in bed."

In bed. She could see the two of them there so clearly. She could feel the excitement. Yet she was terrified, too. "David, I can't jump into anything."

"Sometimes jumping is the fastest way to get the shock over with."

Shock. The shock of finding herself embarking on an affair. That's where they were headed. She'd promised herself she'd never get married again. She'd vowed she'd never put herself in a position where a man could interfere in her life. Hadn't she learned from Jerome there were no happily-ever-afters? She just had to have a simple mindset—hot sex, fun and a role model for her kids. A relationship with David did *not* have to complicate her life.

Famous last words.

Chapter Eight

She couldn't believe she'd won the dessert contest!

Mr. Brolin had called her this afternoon and she still couldn't believe she was going to appear on *The Breakfast Show* taped in New York City early Wednesday morning.

David's hand covered Angela's under the table. "Are you thinking about *The Breakfast Show?*"

"I'm worried I'm going to fall flat in my chocolate!"

Laughing, he reassured her, "No way. You'll get plenty of sleep in that posh hotel room the night before and feel like a queen when the limo picks you up."

"I only hope you are right. They said I can make the torte and send it the day before, then just go through the motions on the set." Angela's gaze strayed toward Anthony who was playing video arcade games across the restaurant.

"I wish he was celebrating with us."

Aromas of tomato sauce, baking pizza dough and Italian wedding soup filled the pizzeria. David sat beside Michael, and Olivia was finishing her pizza beside Angela.

Anthony wasn't sitting at another table, but he obviously wasn't happy, either. He'd eaten his pizza slice as fast as he could, then asked if he could play video games on the far side of the room.

"Can I play a game now?" Olivia asked, wiping her mouth with her hand.

Angela dug into her wallet for quarters.

"I'm going to watch Anthony," Michael decided, scrambling off his chair and going to join his brother.

"Anthony will get used to the idea of us being together," David said with certainty. Anyone she dated would be a pariah to Anthony. "I want the two of you to be able to talk again…to have fun."

"I want that, too, but we can't force him to feel the way we think he should feel. With the holidays coming there are things we can do together. When he sees we're having fun, I think he'll want to be part of that."

"You don't know how stubborn he can be."

After David gave her hand another squeeze, he ran his thumb along her palm and her index finger. Slowly. Sensually.

Her breathing came harder and she could feel her face flushing. "David…" she warned.

"What? You never had a man hold your hand before?"

Had Jerome ever taken her hand like this? Had he touched her so erotically that she'd wanted to hop into bed with him? Not that she could remember.

When she and Jerome had dated, he'd brought her flowers and candy for a while. Their decision to marry had been more practical and convenient than romantic, she supposed. It had turned out that he'd just wanted a woman to cook and clean for him, to have meals prepared when he came home, to make his life easier. For her part, she'd wanted a family, roots, ties and bonds that marriage would provide. It had worked for a time. But after Michael was born and she had to give her attention to three kids, Jerome had turned away. She hadn't known exactly how to get his attention back. Oh, she'd tried the sexy nightie and new perfume and waiting up until he got home from work. But by then he'd shut down. He'd apparently had more than one affair and had liked the variety.

When David intertwined his fingers with hers, he said, "You're a million miles away."

"Not quite a million," she joked, as she looked away from David, noticed Michael tugging on Anthony's arm and realized he wanted a turn, too. She took more quarters from her purse.

When Michael ran over to her she warned him, "Four. That's all."

"You gave Anthony eight."

"He's older than you are. And I gave Olivia six, because she's older, too."

"I'll never catch up," Michael wailed.

Laughing, she turned him in the direction of the video game. "Have fun with what you've got."

David leaned close to her. "You do a great job with them. They listen to you. You can't imagine how many kids I've mentored who don't respect their parents."

"It's gotten easier since they're all out of diapers," she said lightly. "But I've heard the *pre*teen years can turn a person's hair gray, not to mention the teen years." That's when they'd really need a man in their lives—the boys for a role model, and Olivia, so she could learn how to relate to men in a wholesome way. Angela had read all the books. But reading was one thing, being a good parent was another.

"How can you enjoy being here with me like this?" Angela suddenly asked. "You could be having dinner in a gourmet restaurant with a date who could give all her attention to you. You could be in the city. You could be anywhere but here."

When he gazed into her eyes, she could see he wanted to touch her. He wanted to take her into his arms. He wanted to kiss her. With the kids looking over every once in a while, he was playing it cool. She knew he'd get tired of that, too.

"I'm here, Angela, because I like being with you. I like being with your kids. Would I prefer to take you back to my place, slowly undress you and roll around in the sheets until we're both too tired to do anything but sleep in each other's arms? Sure."

The pictures he painted for her made her restless, edgy and altogether dissatisfied with her life the way it was. How could he do that with a few words?

Angela's cell phone played its lilting tune.

"Saved by a cell," David declared with a wry smile.

"I'll just check the caller ID." After she did, she said in amazement, "I have to get this. It's Jerome. Would you mind keeping an eye on the kids? It's too noisy in here for me to hear. I'm going to step out into the corridor."

He motioned toward the machines. "I'll join them."

As Angela moved into the corridor, her heart thumped faster and she remembered what David had asked her. *Are you over your ex-husband?* She had no doubt she was over Jerome, but she wasn't over what he'd done to her and the kids. She wasn't over what he was still doing to their children. As much as she'd like to cut him out of their lives, she knew Anthony and Olivia and Michael needed him. They needed to know their father loved them.

When she answered her call, Jerome seemed surprised that he'd gotten her. "I thought I'd get your voice mail," he said without an introduction. His *GQ*-handsome face had convinced her they'd be "life partners." She'd been disillusioned by that term ever since they'd divorced.

"Did you get my message?" Angela asked. Actually she'd left several.

"That Anthony broke his arm? Yeah, I got it. How is he?"

"He's still upset because you broke your last two dates with him."

"It couldn't be helped. I'm a certified financial planner now and I've been setting up my office in the old Harcourt building. I've been wining and dining clients almost every night. And before you remind me, I know my check is late again. But my capital is going into setting up this office."

Angela wondered how Jerome was paying his bills. Then she realized she didn't have to wonder. His parents had always bailed him out and she suspected they were still doing it.

"The kids miss you, Jerome."

"That's why I'm calling." When he paused, it was a long pause, and dread began to fill Angela.

"I want to take them over Christmas."

"What do you mean you want to take them over Christmas? You want to see them Christmas Day?"

"No, that's not what I mean. I want to take them on a skiing trip. I want to pick them up Christmas Eve and keep them until December twenty-seventh."

"You're kidding. Right?"

"No, I'm not kidding. And to prepare them for the trip and to get used to me again—since it's been a while since I've seen them—I want to take them tomorrow."

"Take them where?"

"I just want to spend time with them," he said lamely. "You said they miss me. I want to see them. What's the problem?"

What indeed *was* the problem? That was obvious. She wanted to spend Christmas with her children…spend Christmas with her children and David.

"I have to think about this. You haven't seen them for two months, and now, suddenly you want to dictate the terms. I suppose this has nothing to do with power and control."

His silence was unnerving until he said with a little bit of that charm back in his voice, "I'm free tomorrow, Angela. I can give them the whole day. Isn't that what you want, too?"

They'd be thrilled with the whole day with Jerome, and she knew it. "All right. I'll give you an answer about Christmas when you pick them up tomorrow."

"Sounds good. I'll get them about one and take them to some burger joint for supper. They'll like that."

Obviously his idea of all day and hers were very different. But, as she'd found out—not soon enough—she and Jerome were very different. "I'll see you tomorrow."

"They're going to have a great time, Ange. You'll see."

She resented him using the nickname Megan had given her. They weren't on a nickname basis anymore.

After she clicked off the phone and dropped it into her purse, she felt terribly unsettled. Entering the pizzeria again, she saw David standing to one side while Anthony battled a machine of his own. Olivia and Michael were sharing another.

David knew there was trouble as soon as he saw Angela's face. The realization hit him full force that she and her ex-husband would always be connected because of their kids. If he and Angela got seriously involved, what would that mean for their relationship? Could he put up with an ex-husband interfering? Could she? It wasn't too late to stop this if he wanted to stop it. After all, they hadn't even had sex yet. He could easily walk away.

However, something about Angela called to him primally and emotionally. He liked her kids, even Anthony, in spite of his attitude. Was he foolish to think if they both handled this like adults, they could at least make the first down?

And then what? the voice of reason asked.

Hell if he knew. He didn't have a playbook for this one.

When Angela reached him, she didn't say anything. That wasn't good.

"What's up?" he asked casually.

"I can't talk about it here." Her gaze went from her kids to all the people milling about.

So they didn't talk there, and David found himself stewing about it as Angela withdrew. She pretended, for her kids, that everything was fine. But her eyes didn't twinkle when she smiled and her glances at him were short and evasive. He'd decided touching her when the kids were around wasn't a good idea, but that created distance between them, too, because when they touched, they connected.

At Angela's house she still didn't relax. Hoping Anthony would come around, he was disappointed when Olivia asked him to play a game with her and Michael, and Anthony sat on the sidelines with his GameBoy. Angela joined in the board game, too, but her mind wasn't on the game, and Olivia had to remind her more than once, "It's your turn, Mom."

Finally, the kids went to bed, one at a time, beginning with Michael. Once again, David felt like an outsider. He would have liked to have joined in, maybe read Michael a story while Angela tucked in Olivia. He could push the issue, but he didn't want to create more resentment with Anthony.

Finally Angela came downstairs and he decided to cut to the chase. "Do you want me to stay or do you want me to go?"

"I don't know why you'd want to stay," she said, her voice catching. "You could be dating any one of a hundred women in Rosewood who don't have kids or ex-husbands."

"Only a hundred?" he teased, needing to see if she could keep her sense of humor in all of this.

"Oh, David." She tried to smile, but bit her lip at the same time.

Serious now, he took her by the shoulders and held her. "When you got that phone call tonight, I realized you and your ex-husband will always be connected. But the question is, how are you going to handle it? How am *I* going to handle it? Can we do it without making each other crazy?"

"I don't know. Jerome's hard enough to deal with without me dating."

David pulled her a little closer. "How badly do you want to be with me?"

Her gaze finally didn't evade his. "Badly."

"Then you've got to talk to me. You can't leave me out of the loop."

When she backed away from him, he could see her hesitation. "What?"

"I only talk to Megan about Jerome. She's like the other side of me that helps me keep things in perspective. When I thought about us being together, I only thought about it…physically."

"I don't know if I should be insulted or complimented by that."

She sank down onto the sofa. If he sat down next to her, he'd kiss her. He'd coax her to tell him what was going on. What was making her miserable. But that wasn't any way to start a relationship. "I'd better go. It seems that you have something to work out."

Her head came up and he could see that she hadn't expected that. Then her shoulders straightened. "Fine. Thanks for taking us for pizza tonight."

Picking up the jacket he'd thrown over the back of a chair, he hung it over his arm and went to the door. He had a rock in his stomach, and he knew if he left, they were probably over. But she had to be willing to make some changes, too. Suspecting she'd wanted an easy way out by hitching on to another man was laughable now. Angela was so independent he could see that might be just as much of a problem as needing to be rescued.

He'd just turned the knob on the door when she called, "David, wait."

From her expression he could see calling out to him had cost her, so he didn't make her come to him. He strode back to the living room, then sat down beside her.

Almost whispering, she looked down at her hands in her lap. "I'm afraid to let you in."

"Because of your husband's affairs?"

"It's not just Jerome."

She was obviously having trouble letting her walls down so he prompted gently, "What else?"

After a long hesitation, she plunged in. "I told you my parents divorced. Well, it didn't happen until I was sixteen. When Megan came to live with us, we both thought we had the perfect family…the perfect parents. Then, overnight, we learned my dad had fallen in love with someone else. Seventeen years of marriage gone in the blink of an eye. He just wanted out. He didn't care about mom *or* us. Only about the new woman. If two people love each other for that long, how can it just end?"

"I don't know. Maybe they stopped working at it."

Considering everything she'd told him, he asked, "Are you telling me you don't trust men to be faithful? Or are you telling me you don't trust them to stay?"

"Maybe both. And if we're starting out with three kids and an ex-husband on the cons side of the column—"

"*One* kid and an ex-husband. The other two seem to like me."

She looked a little angry. "How can you be so… so…cavalier about this?"

"I'm not. But I also believe if we don't keep a sense of humor, it makes problems worse. It makes communicating harder."

After a long, silent moment, when she studied him excruciatingly carefully, she admitted, "Megan says I need to laugh more. She says I signed away my sense of humor with my divorce papers."

He had to smile. "I don't think that's quite true. You probably just need more people than Megan around you to help you decide there's something to smile about."

"I get so caught up in working and being—"

"A Super mom," he filled in. "I know." He pushed her hair behind her ear and caressed her cheek.

It was as if his touch opened a portal inside her. He could see the change in her eyes…the opening of the door…the vulnerability she didn't want to show.

"Jerome wants to take the kids skiing over Christmas," she explained. "He wants to pick them up Christmas Eve and bring them back the twenty-seventh. I've *never* spent Christmas away from my kids. I love seeing their faces Christmas morning, the magic sparkle in their eyes. Anthony doesn't believe in Santa Claus anymore, but Olivia still wants to. And Michael…I just can't imagine Jerome putting him to bed on Christmas Eve, reminding them all about the true meaning of Christmas, reading them the Christmas Story. I want them *here*."

"But you want them to spend time with their father, and you want Jerome to feel like a dad. Right?"

"You're going to give me the man's perspective on this, aren't you?" she grumbled.

"That depends. Do you need me to give it?" When she was silent, he stepped in again. "You know, Christmas is just a date on the calendar. You could start a new tradition. You and the kids could open your presents on Christmas Eve."

"That's not the same."

"As watching Michael still believe in Santa Claus? No. That might last another year. But this year, Jerome could see that magic happen. And maybe it'll help him be a better dad."

"But if they're going on a ski trip, he won't even have a tree!"

She ducked her head into her hands and rubbed them over her face. "Okay. I'm being unreasonable. I'm just having trouble with this. Besides having them with him for Christmas, he wants them tomorrow. He won't tell me what he's going to do or where he's taking them."

"Maybe it's a surprise. Maybe he's going to take them to buy a present for *you*."

"You're bound and determined to see the sunny side of this, aren't you?" she asked with a slight smile.

"I can't take the credit for that this time because I'm thinking selfishly. If Jerome takes Olivia and Michael and Anthony somewhere tomorrow, I'll have time alone with you."

"And what might we do with this time alone?" she asked coyly.

"We could go ice skating."

She blinked.

David couldn't help laughing at her expression. "If it were up to me, I'd take you out to my car and make love to you now. But if I did that, I know you'd still have an ear open for the kids. Even tomorrow, your mind might be partially on them. Ice skating will help us ease into whatever else happens. Meanwhile," he said, sliding his arm around her and drawing her to him, "we can practice making out to see how much we like it."

After a deep, long, wet kiss, he broke it off and stood, grabbing her hand and pulling her up with him. "Now let's go to the breezeway and do that again."

"The breezeway?"

"Yeah. We'll have a door between us and the kids. If they try to open it, at least we'll hear them."

"The breezeway?" she asked again, laughing, as he tugged her toward the foyer, through the dining room and into the kitchen. Three kids didn't have to inhibit them. In fact, being inventive could add spice.

As they were about to find out.

"Whose idea was it to go ice skating today?" David asked with mock sternness as he followed Angela into the breezeway and she dropped her ice skates into a plastic bin.

"It was yours," she said with a laugh, going to the kitchen door and unlocking it.

They'd had a wonderful afternoon. But she didn't know what was going to happen next. She was nervous and excited and felt like a kid on Christmas morning.

Christmas.

She wasn't going to think about it. Her kids had been

so happy to see Jerome this afternoon. So thrilled he was going to take them somewhere. She'd taken Jerome aside and agreed to have him pick them up on Christmas Eve.

David had been right. She had to put her own feelings aside and encourage Jerome to be the father she knew their children needed.

Once inside the kitchen, she turned to David. "It was your idea to go skating. Are you having regrets?"

She didn't have one. They'd driven out to the community pond and had a blast, skating singly to get their feet under them, and then, together. They'd moved as one. She'd been amazed how right it had felt to be with David. He'd kissed her in the gazebo as they'd taken a break from skating to simply absorb the Norman Rockwell scene and feel the holiday spirit. He'd rubbed noses with her as they'd sat on a bench to take off their skates. He'd kissed her again in the car before their drive back to the house, and they'd steamed up the windows until they couldn't see out.

Not once this afternoon had she asked herself what she was doing. Because she knew. She was having fun. She was letting her attraction to David become more than a dream. She was letting him in.

Now he unzipped his jacket and then unzipped hers, too. "No regrets. Except that I didn't wear long underwear. Don't you have any body parts that are frozen?"

"Not any important ones," she joked.

His laugh rumbled through her as he slid his arms under her jacket and around her waist, bringing her close…merely holding her.

His heat became hers. Any parts of her body that had been cold were warming up fast. The laughter in his eyes transformed into something else entirely—a hunger that sent her pulse racing much faster.

"What?" she asked.

"Do you realize we're all alone in this house?"

She hadn't been alone with David like this since the moment she'd met him. Even Megan's car was gone, so Angela knew there'd be no interruptions from her, either. They were as alone as they were going to get. "Maybe we should light a fire, put on some music and enjoy the quiet."

"My fire's already lit. How about yours?" His brows arched as he waited for her answer.

Angela blushed. "I'm…I'm at a loss as to what to say or do. And when you're holding me this close, I can't think."

His voice turned husky. "Is thinking really what you want to do right now?"

"No. And talking isn't, either," she admitted boldly, amazed she was being that honest.

"I think this is the right time for kissing." He touched his lips to hers, but didn't stay there. Next he kissed her chin, then her neck.

"Oh, David."

"I don't want to rush you," he murmured between kisses.

"You're not rushing me. You're turning me on, big-time."

At that he laughed, pushed her jacket from her shoulders, then let his drop to the floor, too.

Night after night as she'd tossed and turned restlessly in her bed, she'd imagined David's naked body. Now she couldn't wait to touch it. Dragging his flannel shirt from his jeans, she began unbuttoning it.

His hands tunneled under her sweater and their arms tangled. They laughed as he pulled it up and over her head.

"We've got a few choices," he determined, his breathing becoming more ragged.

"What kind of choices?" she asked absently as finally she got his shirt unbuttoned, only to find a T-shirt underneath.

"There's the kitchen floor, the dining room table, the sofa or—" he paused for effect "—your bed."

"It's the same bed Jerome and I slept in. I don't know if—"

"Forget the bed." He nibbled at her earlobe, then tickled it with his tongue and sucked on it.

Moaning, she probably would have collapsed at his feet, but he scooped her up into his arms. "Let's see how far we get."

When he began kissing her, her arms tightened around his neck.

As he came up for air, he muttered, "We at least have to get to the dining room where there's carpet."

She felt younger and freer than she'd felt in years. A few steps into the dining room, he stopped, and set her on the table. "I want to see you naked. Now."

"Only if you get naked, too," she bargained.

"Deal."

But getting naked wasn't quick or easy because they couldn't stop kissing. His mouth was demanding and possessive. Her tongue teased his until his only response was a guttural groan. While they kissed, he unfastened her bra. She raked his T-shirt up from his waistband and finally felt his soft chest hair and taut skin. Somehow he unzipped her jeans, shoved them from her hips. While she wiggled out of them, he pushed off his shoes and dropped his jeans.

She'd worn panties that were a blue, lacy triangle, nothing more. His finger traced the lace along her thigh, and as she trembled, he asked, "Were you thinking about this the whole time we were ice skating?"

"If I admit that, you'll think I'm sex starved."

His grin was wide. "Are you?"

"I don't know. I never thought I was that kind of woman, but since I met you I can't stop thinking about what we'd be like together."

"Then don't you think it's time we found out?"

It was easy to see that he was more than ready. Yet he didn't want to rush her. And he was still giving her a chance to back out.

"What if I...?" She stopped then tried again, "What if I can't satisfy you? What if this isn't as much...fun as you expect it to be?"

Splaying his hands through her hair, he held her head. "Don't think about your marriage. Don't think about anything except you and me, here and now." Then he lifted her from the table.

She wrapped her arms around his neck and her legs around his hips.

"The condoms are in my pocket," he said, lowering her onto the plush green carpet. Stretched out on the floor, his hand cupped her breast.

She plucked at his briefs, wanting them off, and he chuckled. "I thought a woman needed a lot more time to get revved up."

"I'm revved," she admitted, leaning close to him, touching her tongue to his nipple.

He let her have her way for a moment, but then he slid his hand down her back into her panties and pushed them down her legs. "I only have so much self-control."

"Self-control isn't everything it's cracked up to be," she teased and brushed her hand along his navel and into his briefs.

From there, hunger, desire and need escalated. She reached for him and he reached for her. Soft touches became erotic play. Deep kisses kept them coming back for more. She couldn't get enough of him. He couldn't get enough of her. Together, they blazed out of control.

Finally, David slipped on a condom. She welcomed him, needing the fulfillment he could give her, desiring to give him satisfaction as he'd never known. When he thrust inside of her, she took all of him, raised her hips so he could bury himself in her more deeply, and felt renewed as a woman.

"Come with me," David urged her.

She wanted to go with him. She did. But so often Jerome had left her behind.

As if David knew what she was thinking, he claimed her more thoroughly by kissing her, thrusting deeper and filling her with only him. She didn't have any warning. Like a volcano finally awakened, heat and pleasure and bone-shaking tingles exploded over and over again, shaking her, swirling her into an ecstasy that brought tears to her eyes. When David stopped kissing her, her body still vibrated with aftershocks, and she contracted around him again and again. His final thrust tore a groan from his throat as he realized his own satisfaction. She held on to him, feeling a union she'd never experienced before…feeling as if he'd touched something so deep inside of her, she'd never be the same again.

He stilled but didn't collapse on top of her. Rather, he rolled her with him to her side, so they stayed joined. How different that was, too. How wonderfully intimate.

"Oh, David," was all she could say as she kept her eyes closed tight so the feelings would last.

He kissed her cheek. "Why are you crying?"

"Because that was wonderful. *You* were wonderful."

Opening her eyes, she watched the expressions on his face, as he smiled slowly and replied, "I think we were wonderful together."

Together. She was still afraid there couldn't be a term like that for her. "This is a fantasy," she murmured and began pulling away.

Bringing his hands down her back to her bottom, he stopped her. "No, it's not a fantasy. It's real."

"Until the kids come in. Until Megan comes home."

"Don't you think they can be part of the fantasy?" he asked.

At that moment, she realized she'd tumbled over the precipice and had fallen in love with David Moore.

She *couldn't* be in love. Not so soon. Anything that happened this fast couldn't last. Anything that happened this fast had to be sheer craziness.

"You're thinking again." He didn't sound happy about it.

This time when she pulled away, he didn't stop her, but he did ask, "What are you so afraid of?"

"Are you kidding me? What am I afraid of? I got married to a man I obviously didn't know. I've spent three years disentangling myself from him and everything that didn't work between us. And now I've known you less than three weeks, and I've slept with you!"

"I wouldn't call it sleeping."

"I'm not in the mood for jokes right now, David. You know what I mean."

Looking as if he were frustrated with her, but looking determined, too, he grumbled, "I heard trouble came in small packages, and now I know it's true."

Indignantly she grabbed for her panties. "If you want smooth sailing, you've stopped at the wrong house."

Before she could put on her underwear *or* make a getaway, he hooked an arm around her and brought her to him for a long kiss. She knew she should resist. She knew she shouldn't take this road that could only lead to heartache. But then David's tongue was dancing with hers. He was laying her back on the floor again. His hard body seemed to fit hers so perfectly.

The sound of a car engine made Angela freeze. That car was rolling into her driveway. That car probably held her ex-husband and three kids.

When David heard the vehicle he swore. "Cleanup time," he muttered. "I'll grab my clothes and head for the bathroom."

"And if they find me half-dressed?" She was already scrambling away, grabbing for her bra.

"Just tell them you were on the way to the shower."

David was out of the room into the kitchen and on his way to the bath.

Gazing toward heaven, she asked, *What have I gotten myself into?* But she didn't have time to wait for an answer. She heard a car door slam and she still had to find her sweater.

Chapter Nine

Thank goodness there was a delay with the kids coming inside. Angela didn't know what had caused it until she opened the front door and saw their arms laden with packages.

With a wave, Jerome backed out of the driveway, and she wanted to shout, *Wait a minute. Why did you buy them presents before Christmas?*

But he didn't give her a chance. He was gone, and David was nonchalantly striding into the foyer, as if he hadn't just hurriedly dressed. As if *she* hadn't just hurriedly dressed. As if they hadn't been on the floor making love five minutes ago!

"Hey, Coach Moore. Look what my dad got me!" Michael was all grins. With a mighty effort, he waved a fire truck at David.

When Anthony saw David, his smile diminished.

Ignoring him, the nine-year-old took an electronic game from his pocket. "Dad got me this. He took us to the toy store so we could show him what we wanted for Christmas. He said he's going to get us a computer."

Not to be undone by her brothers, Olivia waved a Barbie doll dressed like a princess in front of her mom's nose.

What to do? If she didn't sound excited about the toys and what Jerome had bought them, she'd look like Scrooge.

"I'm going up to my room, Mom," Anthony said, running up the stairs.

"Wait a minute. With Coach Moore here, I thought we could play a board game."

Evading her gaze and David's, Anthony decided, "Nah. I just wanna do this."

Hopefully, Michael looked up at David. "Can we play with my truck instead?"

"Let me talk to your mom for a few minutes, pal."

As Olivia shrugged out of her coat, she handed Angela the Barbie doll. "Maybe Santa'll bring me more clothes for her."

Angela took Olivia's coat and gave her back the Barbie doll.

While she was hanging up her daughter's jacket in the closet, David came up beside her and put his hand on her shoulder. "I can tell you're ready to erupt."

Shaking her head, she said sadly, "He thinks toys can make up for lost time."

"They seemed to, though, didn't they?"

"For the moment. He and I need to talk about this. But if I dial his cell phone, how much do you want to bet it will be turned off?"

"I'm a betting man," David replied easily.

When Angela went into the kitchen, David didn't follow her. Dialing Jerome's cell phone number, knowing he'd still be in the car, she wasn't surprised when his voice mail picked up right away.

Returning to the foyer, she saw that David was peering out the window, lost in thought.

"You lost your bet. He's not answering."

Turning to her, he asked, "Are you going to stay mad all afternoon or do you want to have some fun with the kids?"

There was a note in his voice that made her go on the defensive. "You don't think I have a right to be angry?"

"I think that could be a full-time pastime if you let Jerome get to you."

"I don't want him teaching them different values than I'm trying to teach. It's not right if they think toys can make up for not spending time with him."

Unruffled, David responded, "I'm not disagreeing with you."

"No. But you're trying to make some kind of point. What is it?"

He hesitated only a moment. "Do you want honesty or do you want me to gloss this over?"

"I want honesty."

"All right. The truth is—you have no control over what Jerome teaches them. Not unless the two of you can talk about it. And if he won't talk, that ties your hands. The way I see it, you have two choices. You can get angry every time he does something you don't want him to do, or you can make the best of it."

Uncomfortable with David's analysis, she felt as if he was sitting in judgment over her.

"You said you wanted me to be honest." His voice was gentler.

"I don't need advice." Every time she looked at David she remembered exactly how he'd touched her...how she'd touched him. How they'd kissed. How they'd made love on the floor.

"Coach Moore, come see the ladder. It reaches up to the top of the sofa."

"All right, Michael," he called back.

At the sound of Michael's eager voice calling to David, Angela's anger deflated. "I don't want Jerome to ruin the time I spend with you. We didn't have time to...to—"

"Float back to earth?" He traced her lower lip with his thumb.

"David, I can't make Jerome go away."

"No, I guess you can't."

"Are you sure you want to stay?" She suddenly realized how much David was beginning to mean to her. She had definite feelings for him that had intensified as they'd made love. *Had* they made love? Or had they had sex? Wasn't it too soon to even consider being in love?

How could a relationship with David ever work with Jerome intruding? With their lack of available time to spend together?

"I planned to spend the day with you, Angela." David's eyes were warm with amusement. "Who knows? Maybe later we'll even have time to make out."

He was reading her thoughts and teasing her about them. She had to find her sense of humor again. She had to realize a bump in the road didn't have to throw her off the road altogether.

Maybe David saw that more clearly than she did.

Glancing upstairs to make sure Anthony was nowhere in sight, she rose up on tiptoe and kissed David on the cheek. "I'll try to forget about Jerome for the rest of the evening. But he's always going to be part of my life. I'm not sure how that fits in with us."

"We'll figure it out," David promised her, and she almost believed him.

Midmorning on Monday, Moore's Sporting Goods was doing a robust business because of Christmas. One customer after another examined baseball bats and gloves, radar detectors and sometimes anything David and his clerks suggested that might be an appropriate Christmas present. Usually when David was in the midst of the Christmas rush, that was all he thought about. But tonight he and Angela were taking the kids caroling, and he found himself wondering if Anthony's attitude would change. If Angela would push him away if it didn't. If they'd get a few minutes alone. He knew all the signs pointed to a train wreck where Angela was concerned. Yet instincts—and lust, he had to admit—urged him to spend time with her.

After he'd waited on a woman who had insisted men were just too hard to buy for, Edgar pointed to a customer in the fishing tackle aisle. "You might want to take that one."

To David's surprise, he saw the customer was his father! Why had his dad driven here when he'd just seen him last weekend? There had to be a problem, because his father didn't make drop-in visits.

"Dad. What are you doing here? Is something wrong?" David could count on one hand the times his father had visited his store.

Giving up all pretense of checking out the merchandise, his dad said, "There's something I want to talk to you about and I didn't want to do it over the phone."

Another customer came in and his father's brow furrowed. "I guess you're too busy to get away for a cup of coffee. I wasn't thinking about Christmas when I drove down here this morning. You do good business."

David saw Edgar was with a customer. Others were milling about. "If you give me fifteen minutes, I have another clerk coming in at eleven. If you want to go to my place, I could pick up lunch."

"No, I've got to be getting back. I'll occupy myself till your help gets here."

Fifteen minutes later, David was downright worried. Could his dad have a medical condition he hadn't told anyone about? Had something happened with his sister? He distractedly waited on customers, keeping his eye on his father.

Finally his clerk arrived, and he motioned his dad to his office. "I have brewed coffee in here. Unless you really want to go out."

"No. This is fine."

David's office was small but had the essentials—a hutch with a computer and printer, file cabinet, a swivel desk chair and an old wooden captain's chair.

"Have a seat," David offered as he poured two mugs of coffee. "What's on your mind?"

Handing his father the black coffee, thinking that that was one thing they had in common, he waited.

His father looked down into the mug, took a tentative sip, then raised his eyes to David's. "I think it's time for me to sell the farm."

Nothing could have surprised David more. "Is this a decision you've already made or one that's in progress?"

"I've made it, I guess. I'm just getting too old and too tired to handle it on my own anymore. There's a retirement village about ten miles down the road. I went and looked at it. It's not bad. I might get claustrophobia at first, but I'll get used to it."

The retirement village his father spoke of was made up of small cottages and an apartment complex. "You don't sound happy about this."

"Happy?" His father let out a huge breath. "Happy doesn't have anything to do with it. When I think about what I used to be able to do and I can't do now, when I think about the years I had at Cloverleaf with your mom, and growing up there as a kid, I can't imagine leaving it. But we both know, financially, it's just not feasible for me to stay there. I can't keep up with the outside work anymore. You and your sister have busy lives and I don't want to depend on you."

When David thought about his father selling Cloverleaf, sadness came over him that he'd never expected. It was the only home he'd ever known. Letting it pass into someone else's hands wouldn't be easy for him, so he could only imagine how difficult it would be for his dad.

"Does Nancy agree you should do this?"

"I haven't talked to her yet. You're older. I thought you should know first."

After David took a long swallow of coffee, he set the mug on his desk. "Do you want me to talk you out of this?"

Aaron Moore gave him a weak smile. "No, my mind's made up. I just don't see any way around it."

There was a knock on David's office door.

"Yes?"

Edgar opened it a few inches. "Someone's here who wants to talk to *you*. His brother-in-law told him you could outfit him for a ski trip."

"And he won't let you do it?"

"Nope. His brother-in-law told him you wouldn't sell him a lot of stuff he didn't need, just the basics, if you knew that's what he was after."

"It's okay, son," his father said, standing. "I said what I had to say."

To Edgar, David suggested, "Tell the customer I'll be a few minutes. If he wants to wait, that's fine. If not, he can call and make an appointment with me."

Once Edgar was gone, David closed the door again. "I don't want you to feel you have to go. If you need to talk about this more—"

"Nope. I'm done talking. Are you still driving up on Christmas Eve?"

David would love to take Angela to his dad's with him on Christmas Eve. But that might not happen. "I'll be there."

"Good. We can sit down with your sister and Carl, and decide what real estate agency would be best. I won't take up any more of your time now."

"If you need my time, it's yours," David said simply.

After a few moments of silence, his dad rose from his chair, too. "You know, when you opened this store I thought you were making a mistake. I thought coaching kids was the wrong way to keep your hand in football. But I can see now, you like what you're doing. I just wanted to tell you I'm proud of what you've accomplished."

His father was full of surprises today. Until his dad said the words, David hadn't realized how long he'd been waiting to hear them.

"Thanks for telling me that. It means a lot."

His father cleared his throat and went to the door. "Yeah, well, I just want to know you and your sister are happy, no matter how you accomplish it. Any chance I'll see Angela again anytime soon?"

"I don't know. Her life's complicated."

Aaron chuckled. "Whose isn't?"

His father was right about that. Yet with Angela, her emotions were tied up into all of the complications. Was she going to let her kids and her ex-husband be excuses to keep them apart?

If she did, then she didn't care enough, and he was better off living his life alone.

She felt *so* guilty.

Angela loaded the dishwasher, unsure what she should do about David. Since they'd made love, she'd started thinking about tomorrow…a tomorrow with *him*. But Anthony's attitude was keeping her from embracing the idea. He was still giving her the cold shoulder, wouldn't talk to her, wouldn't even look at her. She'd tried to speak with him again before he and Michael and Olivia had gone upstairs to get ready for caroling, but he'd been almost hostile. She knew he was only going along tonight because he'd see some of his friends.

Glancing at the clock above the sink, she noticed that it was six-thirty. David was supposed to be here at six-thirty.

"He'll be here," she murmured to herself.

Unless he'd forgotten. Unless something more important had come up. Unless the whole situation with Anthony wasn't something he wanted to take on. Not long term, anyway. What better way to send her a message than to not show up?

She went to the foot of the stairs and called up to the boys' room. "Michael, are you putting on the green sweater over the tan shirt?"

He came running to the top of the stairs, hair sticking up all over, half his shirt collar under the sweater, half of it out.

She had to smile. She always had to straighten something.

"Is this the one?" he asked.

"That's the one. Look for those heavy, black socks in your drawer so your feet don't get cold."

With a grin, he ran back to his room.

She checked her watch. Five minutes later than the last time she'd looked. The neighbors were meeting at Rebecca and Joe's at seven-fifteen. A few neighbors from the side streets connected to Danbury Way were coming over, too, so everyone could get a copy of the song sheet.

After Angela slipped on her boots, she went to the living room and absently picked up toys. Olivia's new Barbie doll and princess paraphernalia were strewn across the coffee table. Angela scooped it into the vinyl bag on the sofa that Olivia kept for Barbie and her belongings. After she plugged in the Christmas tree lights, she checked her watch again—six-forty-five.

She'd positioned kindling and new logs on the grate in the fireplace when she heard a car in the driveway. Megan had gone to Greg's house tonight as soon as she'd gotten home. They were planning the final details of their

wedding. Their ceremony would take place in a beautiful church in the oldest section of Rosewood. Their re-
ception at the country club afterward would be tasteful
and extravagant. Greg wanted Megan to know he was
proud and thankful to be taking her as his wife. Since
Carly, his ex-wife, had found love on her own and was
blissfully happy with Bo now, she and Bo would even be
attending. Once friends, she and Megan had had a heart-
to-heart. Carly knew Megan had never been the other
woman, that her marriage to Greg had self-destructed on
its own with a lot of help from both of them. Now she
was simply glad that Greg had found someone to
complete him the way Bo completed her.

Weddings. Bridal gowns. Engagement rings.

As she went into the kitchen, Angela shook her head as
if she were shaking the pictures out of it. What she ought
to be thinking about was her spot on *The Breakfast Show*
and how she was going to calm her nerves when she got
into New York on Tuesday night. The show was putting
her up at a five-star hotel and then sending a limousine to
take her to the broadcast. She'd actually be demonstrat-
ing a cooking segment. She'd made the torte last night and
frozen it, so she'd have a perfect one to show to the
audience.

When the kitchen door opened, she waited, half expecting to see Megan walking in, telling her she forgot
something, or that she wanted her advice on a wedding
detail. But Megan didn't walk in. David did.

The relief she felt was overwhelming. "I didn't think
you were going to come."

"I would have called if I couldn't come. I got tied
up at the store. I was about ready to leave when a

questionable return came in—" He stopped. "You seriously didn't think I was coming?"

She felt foolish now. After all, he was only twenty minutes late. But she'd spent many a night waiting for Jerome to come home to dinner, and he'd never showed.

She went into the living room and as David followed her, he unzipped his jacket, shrugged it off and laid it on the sofa. Then he approached her. "Where are the kids?"

"Upstairs, getting ready."

"Why didn't you think I'd come?"

She wanted him to kiss her, but she knew he probably wouldn't take that chance. If Anthony saw them kissing again, he might…he might realize something serious was going on between them.

David was waiting for an answer to his question.

"I thought something might have come up…that you'd found somewhere else you had to be."

Sliding his hand under her hair, he tipped her head up. "I'd rather be somewhere else, all right. In my bedroom or yours."

She glanced toward the stairs.

"*But*…I'll have to settle for freezing my buns off caroling. Before we do, though, I want you to know—"

The front doorbell sounded.

"Are you expecting anyone?" he asked.

Sliding away from his touch, from her need of it, she went to the door. "Nope. Maybe we'll have competition tonight."

When she opened the door, she didn't see Christmas carolers. She saw a teenager, lean, about six feet tall with dark brown shaggy hair, dark brown eyes, baggy pants and an oversize flannel shirt. "Can I help you?"

"I'm looking for Coach Moore. I know he's here. I followed him from the store. I've got to see him."

Trepidation rose in Angela and she wasn't sure what to do. Close the door and talk to David? Let the boy in? Why would he have followed David?

Before she could come to any conclusions, David was at her shoulder. "Hello, Conner."

Now Angela was a little frightened. Conner Waybright was the boy David suspected of burglarizing his store. She looked up at him with questioning eyes. Should she call the police?

"I don't want any trouble," the boy said quickly. "I just…I just wanted to tell you my mom—my mom cried when she got that basket you brought."

"That wasn't from me."

"Maybe not directly, but you had something to do with it. I asked around. I can find these things out. I want to talk to you…alone," Conner said. "I wanted to catch you at your store but you shot out of there too fast."

Leaning down toward Angela, David told her, "I'll just be a few minutes." Then he went outside with Conner and closed the door.

It had all happened so fast, Angela didn't know what to think. She paced for a little while, then finally peered at David and Conner through the living room window. The porch light fell over them. They both looked serious.

Stepping away from the window, she felt as if she were eavesdropping by watching them.

Although it was only five minutes later, it seemed more like half an hour when David came back in. His hair was ruffled from the breeze.

"Is everything okay?" she asked. She heard Conner's car cough, then start up.

"Everything's okay. Conner's the one who stole from the store. He's going to return the merchandise he hasn't sold tomorrow. The rest he's going to work off, starting Saturday."

"You gave him a job?"

"Yep. He needs the money. He stole from me because he was still angry with me. But his family is having hard times. I told him if he likes working at the store, and he's a good worker, he can stay on."

"You don't think he'll steal again?"

"I'll keep a close eye on him. So will Edgar. But I don't believe Conner's a thief. He just needs to earn a little respect and some money, too."

Ever since Angela had learned she'd won the cooking contest, she'd been bouncing around an idea in her head. After she and David had made love yesterday on the dining room floor, it had poked at her again. She needed to know just how involved David was in this relationship. She needed to know just how committed *she* wanted to be.

"I've been thinking," she said softly.

He waited.

"I…" She hesitated. "I was wondering… How would you like to go along to New York with me tomorrow?"

Chapter Ten

"I believe you have a reservation for Angela Schumacher," David said to the clerk at the Kingston Suites Hotel in New York City.

Angela looked around in awe at the five-star hotel's accoutrements, which included a marble-floored lobby, comfortable-looking couches and club chairs covered in damask and velvet, Oriental rugs, fresh-cut flowers and a chandelier that could have lit up all of Danbury Way. The Christmas decorations—wreathes, hundreds of twinkle lights and hand-painted ornaments—simply added to the magnificence of the hotel. David knew the city better than she did, had commandeered a cab from the train station as if he'd done it all his life, had known how much to tip and how to get a bellboy's attention.

He leaned toward her and whispered in her ear. "You'll need ID."

As she pulled her driver's license from her wallet, she wondered what had gotten into her last night. After she'd asked David if he wanted to come along to New York, he'd asked why she wanted him to.

She'd hesitated, because there had been many reasons. She felt safe when she was with him. She felt so alive when she was with him. She'd wanted to share the experience with someone who mattered. So she'd answered, "Because I want to be alone with you."

The answer must have been the right one, because he'd taken her by the hand, pulled her to the living room far away from the stairs, and given her a thoroughly arousing, long, deep kiss. After they'd taken the kids caroling— even Anthony seemed to have a dose of the Christmas spirit as he was quiet at first, then seemed to enjoy singing along—they'd made plans about when they'd go into the city. She felt as if she were embarking on a wonderfully new adventure.

But actually being here, now, with David, realizing she'd taken a giant step that might not mean the same thing to him that it meant to her, she was getting cold feet.

After Angela handed the clerk her ID and he studied it, she noticed a woman come up beside David. She was wearing a lynx coat, carried a Gucci bag, was tall and svelte, maybe in her late twenties. Her arm brushed David's as she waited for another clerk to look up from his computer.

"Sorry," she apologized with a wide smile that made her look not at all sorry.

"No problem," David replied with a slight smile of his own.

Returning his attention to their clerk, David suggested, "We'd like two keys."

The clerk returned Angela's driver's license, then answered, "Certainly."

The brunette beside David turned to him once more. "I'm sorry to bother you. Do you have the time?"

David pushed back the cuff of his leather jacket. "It's 7:10."

"Thank you." She was eyeing him, giving him a come-hither look, and Angela felt like kicking the woman in the shins.

After check-in was completed and Angela was clutching a legal-size envelope the clerk said had been left for her, David guided her toward the bank of elevators.

Since David seemed to know his way around, she asked, "Have you stayed here before?"

"Now and then."

She wondered at what other hotels he'd stayed—and with how many women. After all, he was an eligible single man with football players for friends, not to mention beautiful women ready to line up to date him. Surely he'd taken advantage of that at some point, hadn't he?

"Are you worried about the kids?" he asked, obviously noticing whatever expression had crossed her face.

"No, not really. They like to be around Megan. She lets them stay up later than I do, even when it's a school night. I'll call them later to wish them good night."

The elevator dinged and several men and women stepped off. A few others got on with them, and Angela noticed a redhead in a navy suit, a coat tossed over her arm. She was holding a briefcase and took more than one look at David. He seemed oblivious as he settled an arm around Angela's shoulders. She tensed, not even sure why.

"The clerk said the bellman will be right behind us. Once we unpack, we can go out for dinner, or maybe order room service."

A night on the town or a night with David in the hotel room? Both options gave her enough butterflies to make her queasy. Or maybe it was the high-speed elevator.

The hallways leading to the rooms were as plush and sophisticated as the lobby with their thick, cranberry-colored carpeting, their satin, embossed wallpaper, their credenzas and intimately warm, low-level chandelier lights. When Angela and David arrived at their room, David took the keycard, inserted it until the light turned green, and then opened the door for her.

The king-size bed in a royal blue suedelike coverlet dominated the large room. The furniture was white French country, and the watercolors on the walls comple-mented the theme. The pillows on the bed were more than they'd ever need. Angela's palms became sweaty. Actually, if she admitted it, she was close to panic.

A knock at the door kept her from having to say anything, and she wandered over to the window as David ushered the bellman in, told him where to set the luggage and tipped him.

After the bellman left, Angela took off her coat. "I hope you're keeping track of the tips. I'll have to repay you."

"Forget it." David tossed his jacket on top of his suitcase on its rack in the corner.

He looked exceedingly handsome tonight. He was wearing a sweater with navy and light blue stripes and navy slacks. Handsome, sexy, self-assured.

And she was sharing a room with him…sharing a bed with him.

"What's going through that head of yours?" he asked, as he came to where she was standing at a table for two near the window.

She held on to one of the chairs for support. "I just feel a little out of my comfort zone, that's all."

"I'm ready to order champagne and have a wonderful evening with you. And you're feeling out of your comfort zone?"

"Please don't be angry."

Now he cocked his head and really studied her. "I'm not angry. I'm frustrated. We finally have a chance to be alone and you're putting up barriers. What's going on, Angela? Are you testing me to see how far you can push before I blow up like I did on the football field? Well, push away. Because that's not going to happen again."

Was that what she had been doing? Testing him? If he wanted to talk, well okay, then she was going to tell him what she was thinking. "When I said I was out of my comfort zone, I meant I'm not used to all this. Yet you seem very comfortable. With the hotel, with checking in with me. I just have to wonder how many times you've done this before and with how many women. I have to ask myself what I'm doing here with you as if we're having an affair."

"That depends on your definition of an affair. Does having sex count?"

There was an edge to his voice and she knew he *was* angry. Yet there was so much more than anger there. Sadness, maybe?

"Don't you know I want more than a one-night stand

with you?" he asked sharply. "What do you think is going to happen? We'll go back to Rosewood and I'll forget we were here together tonight?"

"Yes, that's what I'm afraid of! You might want tonight, but what about tomorrow and tomorrow night? I haven't known even one man with staying power."

"Then you've known the wrong men," he returned. "I'm beginning to think *you're* the one who wants the one-night stand so you can preserve control over your life and your kids. You're afraid to give up any of it. If you let someone in, you'd have to do that. I understand independence, Angela, and I admire it. But until you can finally let yourself depend on someone, I'm not sure you have room in your life for me."

The truth in his eyes was too hard to look at. On one hand, she wanted to dive into his arms, let him take her to bed, depend on him in a way she'd never depended on another man. On the other, she was terrified to give up control of her life, terrified to put her children in a situation that might not work out, terrified they'd all get hurt, even worse than they had with Jerome. She didn't want to fail again.

So that meant, what? Not even trying?

Asking David along to New York had been about trying, and look where that had gotten her.

Suddenly David withdrew from her, physically and emotionally. Crossing the room, he picked up his jacket. "I think we both need a little space. I'm going out for a walk."

She wanted him to stay. She wanted to figure this out. But he was frustrated and they weren't getting anywhere.

"I could call room service while you're gone. The food would be here until you get back," she offered.

After a long look at her, he nodded. "A steak would be good."

She hated the distance between them, the miles of territory that just seemed too rough to explore. But if she wanted a relationship with David, she'd have to figure out how to have it.

David returned to the room about five minutes after the food had arrived. While he'd been gone, Angela had called her kids and ironed her outfit for her TV spot the next morning. They'd have to leave the hotel at 4:30 a.m.

That's if David went with her.

They ate pretty much in silence. Every topic seemed to lead back to the two of them, and since they didn't have any answers, they avoided it until dinner was over.

After David pushed the room service table out into the hall, he said soberly, "I think I should get another room for tonight."

If he did that, they'd be over. She didn't want them to be over before they'd begun. "It's a big bed," she murmured. "You don't have to sleep in another room."

His hazel eyes were penetrating as he tried to figure out what she wanted. "When I was in the lobby, I checked with the desk about a late checkout tomorrow. We can leave our things here until you're finished at the studio. Do you want me to go along with you?"

Lord, this was painful. She didn't know what to say next, or do next, or how to make this better. "I'd like that. But it means we won't get much sleep."

"I guess we'd better turn in then." His tone was brusque. "If you want to get changed in the bathroom, go ahead. I'll watch the news."

She was going to have to get up at three-thirty to be ready by four-thirty, so it made sense if they went to bed. The question was—would either of them sleep?

Angela had brought along a silky nightie and robe she had bought for travel. It was easy to pack when she and the kids went to her mom's. The sea-green, silky ensemble was also a lot more alluring than flannel.

When she emerged from the bathroom, David went in, and she felt like crying. Instead, she crossed to the window and looked out at the city, the multicolored lights, the cars honking and zigzagging through the streets. Where had David gone for his walk? What was he thinking? That he was sorry he'd come? That he was sorry he'd gotten involved with her?

She slipped into bed before she heard the water stop running in the bathroom. Minutes later, there he was— bare-chested, muscled, all male, wearing gray flannel sleeping shorts.

Her gaze had been exploring his long, powerful legs when he asked, "Ready for the lights to go out?"

In the dark, Angela was just as aware of David as when the lights were blazing. Maybe more so. Even though the bed was so big, she still felt his weight as he sat on the edge of the mattress. The cover rippled as he slid under it and lay staring at the ceiling. She'd closed the drapes, but a thin ribbon of light from the city that never sleeps filtered between the drawn curtains.

They were on opposite sides of the bed with lots of space between them. She didn't want that space but didn't know how to bridge it.

Then suddenly she did. Turning on her side, she reached out her hand to him. "David."

She felt him turn…felt his hand cover hers.

His voice was husky when he said, "Any women that I dated before you have nothing to do with you. I came to the city often with Duke after rehab. I'd almost died, and I guess I wanted to prove to myself I was still alive, that I could soak in absolutely everything about living. And forget about Jessica."

Although she wasn't sure she wanted to know, she had to ask the question. "Who was Jessica?"

"My fiancée."

Whoa! He'd been engaged. He'd considered spending his life with someone. "What happened?"

In the silence of the room, she could hear the hum of the heating system, a door close down the hall, the elevator bell ding.

Finally he responded, "It's an old story. You said you didn't realize the man Jerome really was until long into your marriage. Jessica had me fooled for while. She knew I had NFL aspirations when we met in college. A week after I was drafted, we were engaged. Then I went to training camp and got hurt."

"She didn't stick by you?"

"She pretended to for a while. I thought her detachment was fear that I'd never be able to walk normally again…that I'd never fully recover. But it wasn't fear, it was disappointment. She broke off the engagement shortly after I left rehab. After all, I was floundering. I didn't know what I was going to do with my life. She wanted certainty and a secure future. I couldn't give her that."

"She didn't stick by you when you needed her most."

"That's right. So I haven't looked for anything serious since Jessica."

"Are *we* serious?" Angela asked, almost tentatively.

"You tell me."

"I'm afraid, David."

"I know you are."

Slowly he intertwined each one of his fingers with hers and curled them into her palm. Then he gave a slight tug on her hand and she didn't know if she moved first, or he did. But in moments they were together in the middle of the big bed and he was holding her. Lying face-to-face, he encircled her with his arm. His hand stroked her shoulders, then down her back. When he kissed her, she became dizzy with the need that had scared her since she'd met him.

Tonight there wasn't room for fear. There was only room for David…and the pleasure they could give each other…the bonds they were forming.

While they kissed, he rolled onto his back, bringing her with him. Stretched on top of him, she could feel every hard plane, every taut muscle, his arousal that was hard and hot against her. Now with both hands, he pulled up her nightgown and explored bare skin from her waist over her buttocks down her thighs. After all her thirty-one years, she finally knew what swooning meant. His hands were large and sensually erotic as he stroked her, then shifted her beside him once more so he'd have access to her breasts.

"Take off your nightgown," he commanded huskily in the dark.

He didn't help, but he watched in the shadowy murkiness of the room. After she dropped it on the floor, she sat before him, naked, and felt free in that. So free…as he pulled off his briefs and they sat in bed facing each other. Throwing pillows to the headboard, he leaned against them, then tugged her toward him until she straddled him. His arousal pushed at her, but he didn't enter her. After he took her face in his hands, he kissed every inch of it. She was writhing, restless and consumed by need, but he didn't join them. He didn't stop. He teased her tongue until it came out after his, and then he sucked on it. Meanwhile, his hands were busy caressing her breasts and she felt as if she were going to come apart into a million pieces.

When his mouth finally broke from hers, she murmured, "David, I need you."

"I need you, too. But I don't want you to forget tonight. I don't want it to get lost when you're running errands and taking care of the kids and working. You're a beautiful, sensual woman, Angela, and you deserve to be treated like one."

The more he kissed and touched her, the more she knew she needed him in her life. He not only excited her, revved up her hormones and made her *feel* beautiful, but he gave her balance and filled the part of her heart that had been hungry and empty for so many years. Their foreplay seemed to last for hours, but she loved every minute of it. She loved touching him as intimately as he touched her. She loved the texture and scent of his skin…his chest hair tickling her cheek…his arousal that was hot and pulsing and told her just how much he needed her.

When she rubbed her cheek against him, teased him with her tongue, he sucked in a breath.

"Do you like that?" she purred.

"Too much. You do that too long and the fireworks are going to go off."

"I might like to see that," she teased.

"I think you'd rather feel it," he countered, rolled her onto her back, then reached into the nightstand drawer.

David entered her with a long, powerful thrust that took her breath away. Grabbing on to him, she never intended to let go. As he rocked against her, she wrapped her legs around his hips, meeting his thrusts, igniting passion that had been buried and now came alive. The first time they'd made love had been fun and quick and frenzied. This time…this time was *so* different.

This time was soulful and deep and heartfelt. As the tension inside of her coiled tighter and tighter, she held her breath. David kissed her, thrust deeper, and the colors burst like millions of colored twinkle lights over the city, bright against the darkness, lighting up her world. She was still embracing the beauty of it when his release came. Together, they floated into that never-never land where lovers are one, and passion and satisfaction overtakes the mind and the body and the soul.

Staying joined together, he rolled them to their sides. "I didn't think it could get any better than the first time. I was wrong."

"We'll never be able to top that."

"That depends on how much sleep you want to get tonight."

"We have to be up so early, it doesn't seem much use to go to sleep, does it?"

In answer, he kissed her. And they started all over again.

* * *

A representative from *The Breakfast Show* met David and Angela at the door to the building, then led them to the third floor where the show was taped. David noticed Angela suppressing a yawn and smiled. They hadn't gotten much sleep. After dozing a few extra minutes this morning, they'd had to rush to get ready. Now as Angela removed her coat, he really looked at her.

The representative from the show disappeared with their coats, and he saw anxiety steal over Angela's face. "Hey, you're not getting nervous, are you?"

"Oh, no. I'll just be cooking in front of millions of people. Not nervous at all."

Laughing, he took her by the shoulders. She was wearing a blue sweater and matching wool slacks, and all he could think about was taking her back to bed again. "You look great." He touched the pearl dangling from a silver chain, a diamond winking from it. He fingered the pearl.

"That's my good-luck charm," she said softly. "My mother gave it to me for my sixteenth birthday before everything blew apart. I remember how she was then. It gives me hope that maybe someday we can be close again. Maybe that's just wishful thinking."

"There's nothing wrong with wishful thinking. She'd be proud of you, if she could see you. Did you tell her about this?"

"I left a message, but she didn't return my call."

The young intern came back to them and put her hand at Angela's elbow. "Time for you to go to makeup and meet the host. We have the torte you froze and messengered to us yesterday. It's in the refrigerator. It looks wonderful."

The intern motioned David to the chairs for the audience. "You can sit anywhere you'd like. Things will start hopping in another fifteen minutes or so."

"Since you're going to do makeup all over again…" David joked. He took Angela's hand, brought her to him for a short but thorough kiss, then murmured, "Good luck. You'll do great."

When David went in search of a cup of coffee, he was invited to share in a breakfast of doughnuts. Passing time, he talked to members of the staff for a bit. Finally he migrated back to the chairs, thinking about last night. Thinking about Angela. Thinking about going back to Rosewood.

Distracted, he'd almost finished his coffee when a man in a cable-knit sweater, his face familiar, came to join David. "Hi, there. I'm Bart Seward. Aren't you David Moore?"

Now he recognized the man. He was the sportscaster for *The Breakfast Show.* "Yes, I am."

"What are you doing now? I heard about that godawful accident. Are you here to interview for my job?" the man asked, semi-facetiously.

"Your job's safe. I own a sporting goods store and I coach high-school football. I came with Angela Schumacher. She's doing the cooking spot today."

"Oh. The winner of the contest. Yeah, I met her. She's a bubbly little thing. If she can hold on to that on the air, she'll be a hit. Fifteen minutes of fame could turn into a bigger opportunity."

"What do you mean?"

"You never know who's watching the show. If she has charisma, if she has something a producer likes, someone might grab her for a sitcom deal. Who knows, these days? Or a reality show."

"That doesn't happen very often."

"More often than you think. The higher-ups are always looking for the next big trend. Or someone who can grab an audience. Yeah, it's the exception, but it happens."

The sportscaster stuck out his hand. "Anyway, it's good to meet you."

"You, too."

The taping of the show was interesting to watch, but David's mind was only half on it until it was time for Angela's segment. He moved to the area with the kitchen set.

Last night he'd seen Angela's note cards lying on the desk—the one-two-three of her demonstration. But now she didn't even look as if she needed a teleprompter as she explained to the host how to make the torte…as she laughed with him about the aphrodisiac quality of chocolate. She absolutely sparkled. He could see her face on the monitors, her silky hair sliding against her cheek, her eyes growing big with delight, her smile lighting up the set. If anybody could be a hit, *she* could be.

David remembered his few days in the spotlight and how he'd shied away from it. Angela seemed to embrace it. What would happen if *she* was offered a job from this? Would she move away from Rosewood? Would she take her kids from their school and friends and start over? Last night she'd admitted how scared she was to let him in.

Trust was an issue for both of them. While Angela had memories to bury of what Jerome had done to her, David had to wonder if *she'd* stick around if the going got tough. He knew her kids had to come first. But would she let them dictate her life? Would she let them dictate their relationship?

That was one thing he wouldn't stand for. The kids had to be considered, but as adults, he and Angela had to make the decisions. Could he become part of their family or would he always be separate? Would he always be resented? Had he started something that was only going to bring all of them heartache?

He hoped not.

Angela had caught sight of him. In spite of the lights, she seemed to look directly at him when she said, "The kitchen can be the heart of the home. As a mom, I want to make it a place where my children can talk about their day and tell me anything that's bothering them. I've got to admit, because of working, I can't cook as much as I'd like. Not the fancy things like this torte. But every day I cook something to bring us all together in one place at the same time. I think that matters."

David knew it mattered, just as Angela's Super mom status was important to her. But how important? Would Angela consider taking off her Super mom hat? Was she satisfied to be simply his lover?

Being lovers wouldn't be simple at all. He wanted more than that…a whole lot more.

Chapter Eleven

"They really loved my torte," Angela said for about the hundredth time.

David had to chuckle. They'd taken the train back to Rosewood and now picked up his car at the station to drive home. "I don't know why you're so surprised. You're a good cook."

"But they loved everything about it, from the white chocolate trim to the holly leaf decorations. Trent Jamison actually said it was the best chocolate dessert he'd eaten in years."

The host had flirted with Angela just enough to make the segment fun, and David had been surprised to realize he'd been jealous of the man. "Trent liked *you,* Angela. Everyone liked you. It wasn't just the torte."

She glanced at him now, obviously perplexed.

"You absolutely radiated warmth and friendliness

from that kitchen set, and I'm sure it got to the viewers. That's what everyone was responding to."

"Once I got started, I forgot I was nervous," she admitted.

As David took a turn that would lead them to the west side of Rosewood, he noticed Angela look out the window and frown.

"What's the matter?"

With a sideways glance at him, a guilty flush stole into her cheeks. "I was just thinking how great it was to be away for a day." Then she added, "To be with you."

David had thought that once he and Angela had sex he could maneuver his brain and his body parts back in sync. Whenever he touched her, whenever she touched him, whenever she smiled at him a certain way, no matter whether they were with the kids, in a TV studio or in a hotel room, his body reacted. He'd never had that disconnect before—that his brain couldn't control the rest of him. And it was damn disconcerting. Now it was happening again, and he knew exactly what she was thinking. Once they were in Rosewood, once they were back with her kids, their time alone would be extremely limited. They'd be lucky if they could sneak a kiss, let alone a quickie. Speaking of quickies—

"Which part of being alone did you like most?"

She was into a full blush now. "Do you have to ask?"

Dusk was falling and David made a sudden decision. "Is Megan expecting you at a specific time?"

"No. I told her I didn't know what train we'd be catching. Why? If we check into a motel, everyone in Rosewood will know it," she teased.

"Yep. A motel won't work. But Lovers' Lane might. Are you game?"

At first she looked astonished at the idea. Then she grinned. "What if we get caught?"

"The Rosewood police are too busy watching for Christmas decoration vandals. But if you don't want to risk it—"

"Let's do it," she replied in a whisper, and he had to grin. He doubted if Angela had given in to this sense of adventure in a long time. He hadn't, either.

Lovers' Lane wasn't more than a dirt trail through a section of publicly-owned woods. The end of it emerged onto an overlook near the reservoir. But that wasn't where he was headed.

They didn't talk as he found the turnoff for the trail. He wondered if excitement was growing for Angela the same way it was growing for him. Literally.

"I've never done anything like this," she confided in a low voice, and he thought he heard her words tremble a little.

"Not even as a teenager?"

"I started dating about the time my parents divorced and then I stopped. I saw what my mother was going through with my dad and I didn't want any part of a relationship that could tear me up like that. I met Jerome when I was taking courses at the community college, and he always preferred...a bed."

"Beds are okay. I think we proved that. But there isn't always a bed around if a couple wants to be spontaneous. We proved that, too." He remembered every minute of their lovemaking on the dining-room floor.

He heard her shift on the seat and wondered if the tingles of sexual anticipation were already racing through her body the way they were racing through his. Finally,

David saw what he was looking for—an area off the side of the road that had been cleared of fallen trees.

"Have you been here before?" Angela asked.

"I've driven through here before. I've never brought a woman here, if that's what you're asking." Leaving the SUV running, he unfastened his seat belt and opened his window a crack. "Come on. I'll get a flashlight and we'll crawl into the backseat."

"David?" she asked hesitantly before he was out of the car.

He poked his head back in. "What? Are you having second thoughts?"

"No. I just…I just feel like I'm breaking the law or something."

He laughed. "That depends on how many clothes we take off. You know, indecent exposure and all. But if no one sees us but *us*—" He brushed her hair from her cheek and ran his thumb over her lips. "I can't wait to kiss you. I can't wait to be inside you again."

Her lips parted. Her breaths came faster. Then she whispered, "I'll meet you in the backseat."

David adjusted the front seat to give them more room in the back.

When he slid toward Angela on the bench seat, she giggled. "I can't believe we're doing this."

"We're not doing anything…yet," he said drily.

Unbuttoning her wool jacket, he tucked his hand inside at her waist. "Hmm. Nice and warm here." She was still wearing the blue outfit she'd worn for her demonstration, and he could feel the heat of her skin through the soft sweater. He also felt her tremble. "Cold or excited?"

"Excited," she admitted, unzipping his parka, lifting his sweater from his hips, pulling his shirt from his khakis. When her hands touched his bare skin, he was already on fire for her.

"How fast do you want to go?" he asked, kissing her neck.

"I can keep up with you," she insisted.

He gave a wry chuckle. "I don't know. I'm pretty primed right now."

"And you think I'm not?"

Those words hit him as the sexiest he'd ever heard. He kissed her, and it was all tongue, deep angles and hunger that had to be satisfied right now.

Breaking away, he tore off his jacket, folded it and shoved it behind her, close to the door, so it would act as a pillow.

"How are we going to do this?" she asked unsteadily, leaning back against his coat.

"Any way we can." He tunneled his hands under her sweater and caught her breasts in his hands. She moaned as he kissed her nipple, unfastened her slacks and slid his hand inside.

"I don't need much," she whispered against his neck breathlessly. "I want you—"

Her breath caught as his fingers found the swollen nub and she climaxed, suddenly, and to his mind a little too quickly. Her orgasm didn't last long, and now he said, "Let's give that another try."

Sliding away from her on the seat, he opened his belt buckle and unzipped his fly. Then he swore. "Damn it. I have to use a condom. Hold on a minute."

"Can I help?" Her voice was trembling, and he could see she wanted this as much as he did. "Wallet, back pocket," he got out.

After she took his wallet from his slacks she found a condom with the bills. "Let me do this," she offered.

He'd intended to leave his slacks on, but now he changed his mind. He undressed as she flipped off her shoes, pushed down her slacks and panties. Leaning over him, she touched her tongue to his arousal and he almost leaped off the seat. "Oh, no. Not this time. We'll save that for when I have more…control."

He lay the burning flashlight on the floor so they could see what they were doing, as well as see each other.

Now she smiled at him. "I'm going to get you back for all that pleasure you gave me last night."

"Just remember, the car's running, and someone wanting to see the town's Christmas lights could be going by to the overlook."

"That makes this even more exciting," she admitted, resting the condom on his erection, not rolling it down quite yet.

"Angela," he warned, laughing.

Finally she rolled the condom over him. "Now what? Should I—?"

Before she could even ask, he'd circled his arm around her and lifted her onto his lap. She was such a little bit of a thing. But she was all woman, and he didn't even know if she knew that.

"Some men don't like women to be on top," she whispered, as she slid forward a little and her petals opened for him.

"I'm not some men," he growled, pushing into her, wrapping his arms around her, tugging her close. "Damn, but you feel good!"

"I doubt if anything is going to happen for me again. I mean—"

"Something's going to happen for you again. I'm not going to have this fun all by myself." Caressing her bottom, he rocked against her, pushed deeper, found physical satisfaction with Angela that he'd never found with another woman. Maybe because it wasn't only physical. Maybe because the physical act itself represented what was happening to them emotionally. So she worked two jobs and had kids—including a son who didn't like him very much right now. If they stood together, if they decided they wanted this, they could make it all work. Couldn't they?

A voice he didn't want to recognize, chanted in his ear, *If Angela can stick it out.*

He ignored the voice and went for the pleasure.

Sliding his hand between them, he touched her and he knew she was going to climax again. She cried his name, not even attempting to muffle it. He found release and fulfillment seconds later, shuddering into her, holding on to her, aware of the midnight darkness around them, the cocoonlike feel of being alone in the woods with no one around for miles.

When she lifted her head, he kissed her, knowing he could do this again and again and still not have enough of her. But right now, his SUV was burning gas and they still had to get back into Rosewood.

Breaking away slowly, he let her lips cling to his. Then he leaned back a few inches.

"That was…stupendous," she said, smiling.

"And now we have to come back to earth," he said soberly. That voice inside his head was chanting again. He knew this wasn't the place for a serious discussion, but at her house they wouldn't have any time for conversation. "Tell me something. If Jerome had been sorry for what he had done, if he'd told you he'd go to counseling, would you have stayed in the marriage?"

She looked surprised that this was what he wanted to

talk about while they were still joined as they were. But after a few moments she answered, "I'm not sure. He broke my trust, David, and I'm not certain that could have ever been fixed. I probably would have tried counseling."

She looked him straight in the eye and asked, "If your fiancée had come back six months later, if she'd said she'd made a mistake, if she wanted whatever life the two of you could find together, would you have taken her back?"

Touché. She'd turned it around on him, and he hadn't expected that. "I don't know. I doubt it. But there is a difference. Jessica and I weren't married. You and Jerome were."

"I'm not sure Jerome got married ever intending to *keep* his vows. For me, I decided that if keeping my vows to Jerome was hurting my children, I had to choose the greater good."

The greater good. Her children would always be the greater good. That was the way it should be.

The chant in his head stopped. Maybe because reality flooded in. The past two days already seemed to be miles behind them.

Peering out the side window, he saw a light snow brushing along the glass. "It's snowing. We'd better get you home."

He saw the recognition in Angela's eyes that their sojourn from day-to-day life had ended and she didn't like it any better than he did.

When Angela entered Latte & Lunch on Friday, she couldn't help but think of the morning she'd met David here. In some ways that seemed so long ago. In others...

Thinking about David brought a flush to her cheeks.

She couldn't believe she'd acted like a wanton teenager in his car the day before yesterday. It had been so much fun. Until he'd asked her about Jerome and she'd returned the question about Jessica.

Molly and Sylvia must have been watching for her because they waved as she headed for the table they'd chosen. It was in a corner near a potted palm and afforded the most privacy the restaurant had to offer.

"Rebecca's going to be a few minutes late," Molly said as Angela joined them.

Molly was nine months pregnant and due anyday. With her long, brown, curly hair, her big brown eyes and a radiant smile, she was the most beautiful mom-to-be Angela had ever seen. She'd married an old friend in September, though he wasn't the father of her baby. But that certainly didn't seem to matter to Adam. He couldn't wait to become a dad and make Molly's child his own. Apparently, some men had the dad gene, whether they were biological fathers or not.

David seemed to have it, too. He was still trying with Anthony, even though her son wanted no part of his overtures...no part of his conversations or jokes. Anthony's behavior caused a strain between them, and she wasn't sure they could overcome that.

Sylvia Fulton, in her late seventies, was an unofficial granny to everyone on Danbury Way. Short and plump, she had beautiful gray bouffant hair, and she usually wore a smile. "Come, sit beside me," she invited Angela. "We haven't caught up in a while. I've been hearing all kinds of rumors, though."

At that moment Rebecca rushed into the coffee shop, and Angela didn't have to comment.

After they all hugged, Molly declared, "It's a shame Megan, Carly and Zooey couldn't join us."

Sylvia, who usually knew everyone's comings and goings, simply replied, "Zooey had to take Jack Jr. to the doctor's. He had an earache. Carly had a meeting at the community center, and I imagine Megan had business obligations."

Angela nodded. "She had lunch with a client. She's definitely tight on time."

"And of course she wants to spend any spare time she can with Greg," Sylvia teased. "I hear you've been spending spare minutes with David Moore. Are you going to tell us all about that?"

"Did you get the football thing straightened out?" Rebecca asked.

Since she'd become friends with each of these women, Angela had always been very open with them. But now she was hesitant to share her private life. Her relationship with David was so fragile, was so new, she was afraid if she poked at it and let everyone inspect it, it might dissolve before her eyes.

Nodding to Rebecca she assured her, "It's all straightened out."

Obviously seeing her hesitancy, Molly suggested, "Why don't you tell us all about New York? We saw you yesterday morning. You did great! Anyone would think you'd been cooking on TV for years."

Laughing, Angela told them about the limo, the host of *The Breakfast Show,* the goings-on behind the scenes.

"And your young man went with you?" Sylvia pressed, apparently determined to find out if Angela was involved with David. But in a kind way, a motherly way, an I'm-just-looking-over-your-shoulder-to-figure-out-what's-best-for-you kind of way.

"Yes, David went with me. He's more familiar with New York than I am. He— It was just nice having someone there to enjoy it all with me." She knew her cheeks had reddened, and the women were probably guessing what else had gone on in New York besides *The Breakfast Show*.

Angela's cell phone rang and, for once in her life, she jumped at the chance to answer it. "Excuse me," she murmured as she pulled it from her purse. Ten minutes later she clicked off the phone and looked at her friends in a daze.

"What is it?" Rebecca asked. "You look shell-shocked."

Shell-shocked was one word to describe it. As the conversation sunk in, Angela realized *off-the-wall-fantastic* was another. "You're not going to believe it."

"Believe what?" Molly asked.

"I've just been asked to audition for a spot on a show that will be aired on the Food Network!" Her voice had risen with each word.

Sylvia cocked her head and tugged on a curl along her cheek that had escaped from the bouffant style. "What kind of show is it?"

"It's called *Meals Across America*. Each day of the week, a homemaker prepares one of the courses. They'd want me to do desserts, which would air on Fridays. But the best part—at least I think it's the best part—is that they want to tape it in my house. They want the shows to originate from the cooks' homes. Can you imagine?"

"But what would you do about your job with Dr. Zef-flinger?" Rebecca asked, always the practical one.

"I don't know. If the food show paid enough, I could possibly work more hours at Felice's Nieces and do the cooking on Fridays."

"Don't they run shows like that as a trial at first?" Molly asked. "Then if the ratings are good enough they continue it—or cut it."

Angela groaned. "I didn't think of that. I don't think Dr. Zefflinger would give me a leave of absence to let me try it."

"You could ask him," Rebecca decided. "What do you have to lose? When's the audition?"

"December twenty-eighth. That's when the crew will descend on my house. The producer said they won't take long to make a decision, because they want to get the show rolling. I'm so excited I could burst! I could work at something I really like doing. He also mentioned that if the show goes over well, there could possibly be a cookbook deal in this."

"We should be having lunch someplace fancier to celebrate," Rebecca added.

"There's nothing to celebrate yet. If the audition goes well and I get a chance to do this, then we can have a celebratory lunch at Entrée." Entrée was a trendy restaurant owned by their neighbors, the Vincentes.

Angela was glad she'd been having lunch with her friends when the call came in. It made everything more exciting. But now she wanted to phone David. She wanted to see David. What would he think about this opportunity?

Since when did she care what a man thought about what went on in her life?

Since she'd met David Moore.

As the women turned Angela's options inside and out,

as they decided what she should wear for the audition and what she should make, time sped by quickly. Angela checked her watch and saw she had to get back to work.

When she stood to put on her coat, Sylvia said, "I'll walk you out, dear. I have to be going, too. I have a garden club meeting this afternoon. We're already discussing what we're going to put in the planters on the square this spring."

After Angela hugged Molly and Rebecca, assuring them she'd see them at Carly's party on Christmas Day, she walked out of the restaurant with Sylvia. Going to the macadam parking area to the side of the restaurant, Sylvia stopped and put her hand on Angela's arm. "The children have their Christmas pageant at church tonight, don't they?"

"Yes, they do. Anthony's a shepherd, Olivia's a lamb and Michael's one of the angels."

"Will Jerome be there, too?"

"I told him about it. I called him and reminded him of the time. I know the kids told him all about it, too, when they saw him on Sunday. But you know Jerome. That doesn't mean he'll show."

"Is your young man going?"

"He's only three years younger than I am," Angela replied, almost defensively.

Sylvia laughed. "Oh, my dear. I didn't mean he was younger than you. I meant he was younger than *me*. Almost everyone's younger than me and Horace these days. I hope you're not worrying about a few years either way. But that isn't what's worrying you, is it?"

"You think something's worrying me?"

"I think you try to do too much."

"You mean this new job opportunity? If I can juggle

everything, if I can make the finances work, it could be the best thing that's happened in a while for me."

"Even better than Mr. Moore?"

"No. Of course not. I mean, that's not even in the same category."

"Having a dependable man in your life could change a lot of things. I know you young women want to do everything on your own. But you simply can't do it all. I don't know how I ever would have managed without Horace. We're partners."

"Not all men know how to be partners."

"You were unlucky with Jerome. You weren't soul mates. Anybody watching the two of you together could tell that. But now you and Mr. Moore…"

Angela narrowed her eyes and stared at her neighbor. "You haven't seen us together."

"Oh, yes, I have. I've seen him help you from his car. I've seen him take your hand as the two of you hurry inside. Irene Dare told me all about the two of you ice skating and kissing in the gazebo."

Irene Dare was a notorious gossip who lived on Maplewood Lane, a street away. She insinuated herself into the Danbury Way goings-on whenever she could, and then loved to chatter about it to everyone she saw.

"You know what happens when Irene tells a story. It gets a lot more detailed than whatever happened in the first place."

"You and Mr. Moore *didn't* kiss in the gazebo?" Sylvia's eyes were filled with mischief.

"Yes, we did, but—" Angela threw up her hands in frustration. "You can't possibly tell we were meant to be together by the way we act with each other."

"Well, of course I can. I can't wait to actually have a conversation with the two of you. If not tonight, then at

Carly and Bo's Christmas party. You are going to bring him along, aren't you?"

"We haven't discussed Christmas yet. He might be spending it with his family."

"I hope I have a chance to officially meet him soon. Now we'd better get into our cars before we freeze our noses off. Have fun tonight with your children at the pageant. They grow up much too fast."

Angela knew that was true. It seemed like only yesterday that Anthony was as young as Michael, and Olivia was in diapers. She was going to miss them desperately on Christmas Day. Tonight she'd ask David what he was doing, and if he wanted to go with her to Carly's party. Last night she'd stayed up late, making him a coupon book of all the meals she cooked best…as well as a few coupons later in the book for a different type of dessert. Tonight, on her way home, she was going to pick up a picture frame for a photo she'd found of her and the kids. She was hoping he'd like it. She was hoping her present would convey to him her deep feelings for him.

Angela and David were seated in the third row of chairs facing the stage in the church's social hall when she told him her news.

"You're going to be a TV star."

She laughed, a bit nervously, he thought. "No, not a TV star. A cook. What do you think about it?"

"I think if it's what you want, you should go for it. Are you going to be able to make it work?"

"That's the question I can't answer yet. Until they make an offer and I know what kind of salary I'd have, until I know if I'm getting a renter or not, until… So many things."

"You *do* know you can't work three jobs." As soon a

he said it, he knew he shouldn't have. Yet someone had to make Angela face reality.

"There are men who work three jobs."

"Not while trying to be Super mom, too."

"You sound like Sylvia," Angela grumbled.

"Sylvia?"

"Sylvia Fulton. She's another one of my neighbors. She told me today she thinks I'm trying to do too much. And just what is too much? Keeping a roof over our heads? Keeping my children in decent clothes? Keeping the car repaired and the utilities paid?"

When David shifted in his seat, his knee grazed Angela's and her gaze shot to his. The current between them was alive and well and raring to go. "Let me ask you something. What would happen if you moved to a smaller place and had to work less so you'd have more time with your kids? Maybe even more time with me."

She looked away from him at the red curtain drawn across the stage, then finally turned toward him again. "Do you want me to sell my house because it's where Jerome and I lived?"

"No. But I think you should consider selling the house if that means your life will be richer, fuller and maybe easier."

The noise from all the parents chattering about their kids and the performance had grown louder. The music director came onto the stage and David knew their conversation had ended for the time being.

Angela looked over her shoulder to the back of the audience. "I don't see Jerome yet. It would be just like him to miss half of this."

Or not show up at all, David thought, but didn't say it. When he'd arrived at Angela's tonight, he'd sat down with Anthony and wished him good luck with his performance.

Anthony had looked him straight in the eye and said, "My dad should be the one taking me and Mom and Olivia and Michael to the pageant. Not you. He just can't get off work early enough so we can get there in time to put our costumes and makeup on. But he's going to be there."

David knew it was a common fantasy for kids to think that their divorced parents would get back together again. He wondered if Angela had ever had that conversation with her three. Whether she had or not, all they could do with Anthony was be supportive and positive and hope they could form a friendship again. David had told the nine-year-old, "I'm glad your dad's going to be there. I'm sure he'll be proud of you."

It had been time to leave then. For Anthony's sake, David hoped Jerome would act like the father the boy needed tonight.

"Maybe you just missed seeing him in this swarm of parents," he reassured Angela now. "Will he try to find you?"

"I don't care if he finds me. Just so he lets the kids know he's here."

The pageant began with the fanfare of a high-school student playing a trumpet. All of the kids did great, from the chorus, to Michael leading a troop of angels. But before, during and after, there was no sign of Jerome. After the pageant, Olivia had asked her mother if her dad had been there.

"I didn't see him, honey. But that doesn't mean he wasn't here."

Anthony didn't say anything as Michael chattered the

whole way home about how the boy in front of him had mixed up all the words to the song.

They'd just gotten into the kitchen when Angela's cell phone rang. Taking it from her purse, she answered it. After a few murmured comments, she said to Anthony, "It's your dad. He wants to talk to you."

Looking unsure, Anthony took her phone. "Hey, Dad. Did you see me in the pageant?"

David couldn't hear Jerome's part of the conversation, but he saw Anthony's expression. The disappointment. The sadness. And this time, anger. "But you *said* you'd be there."

A pause.

"Yes, I know Mom needs you to send her checks." There was another pause. "Okay, I'll see you Christmas Eve."

Closing the phone with a snap, Anthony threw it against the kitchen cabinet. It rebounded and hit the floor.

"Anthony!" Angela exclaimed.

Without thinking twice, David stepped in. "Anthony, that's not acceptable behavior. Pick up that phone and tell your mother you're sorry."

Turning on David, Anthony cried, "I will *not* pick it up. You aren't my dad. You can't tell me what to do." Then he ran through the foyer and clomped up the stairs.

This time David was going to talk to the boy, no matter what Angela said.

Chapter Twelve

Olivia's mouth was still rounded in an *O*.

Michael's eyes were big and wide.

Angela looked as if she'd been body slammed by a defensive lineman. "He's never done anything like that before," she apologized, still aghast.

Without hesitating, David took control. "Olivia, I'm sure you and Michael are hungry after that pageant. Why don't you two have a snack?"

David's words must have propelled Michael into action. After he ran to pick up Angela's phone from the floor, he handed it to her. "Can we have some of those snickerdoodles you made, Mom?"

"Sure." She nodded absently, her gaze on David's.

"I'm going to talk to him, Angela. I can't let him get away with that." He didn't wait for her approval but headed for the stairs.

Angela was right behind him as he went to Anthony's door. He knocked, but the boy wouldn't answer.

When he put his hand on the knob, he found it was locked. "Anthony, open the door. We have to talk."

"There's nothing to talk about."

"I know your dad disappointed you tonight."

"He had work to do," Anthony shouted back. "He's going to buy us a computer for Christmas. I don't need a Big Brother. You just go back to where you came from."

"Anthony, I know you love your dad. And that's the way it should be. I would never try to take his place. There's no reason why we can't be friends. Don't you need a friend?"

Silence answered him.

There was a tightness in David's chest, and he knew that was because he had to solve this thing with Anthony if he and Angela were going to move forward. Turning to her, he said, "You told me when he locked himself in this room before, you opened the door with a shish-kebob skewer. How about getting one for me?"

Angela's shell-shocked look was gone now. Although she still appeared distressed, she shook her head. "No. He doesn't want to talk to you. *I* need to talk to him. I need to explain about Jerome—"

"Explain? What's there to explain? Your ex-husband doesn't know how to keep a commitment."

Moving away from the door to the top of the stairs so Anthony couldn't hear them, David said, "Someone has got to explain to your son that his father has never learned to be responsible. He can't keep blaming himself because Jerome doesn't act like a dad. Let me talk to him, Angela. I think I can get through to him."

"He's shutting you out. I can't let you just go into his room like you belong here—"

Her words were like a physical blow. But he kept pushing because he knew this was a turning point for them. "I either belong here or I don't. You're going to either let me into your life or you're not. I'm not going to walk around the edges of your family, only stepping inside when the right mood hits. I thought we'd gotten further than that."

"I can't…" She stopped, then went on, "I can't put my happiness ahead of Anthony's. Can't you see that?"

Angry now, he couldn't keep his honest estimation of the situation inside. "No. What I see is a woman who won't stand up to her own son. What I see is a mom who thinks love is giving in. You've got to set down some guidelines for Jerome, as well as Anthony and make them both accountable."

Her cheeks flushed. She said, "You make it sound so easy, David. Well, it's not. I'm in the middle—of my kids, of being divorced, of trying to keep it all from falling apart. You can go back to your apartment and forget about it."

"And whose fault is that? I don't forget about it, Angela. You seem to think I'm only in this for the sex. If that were the case, I wouldn't still be here. I'm beginning to wonder if I shouldn't have my head examined for even thinking that this could work." Raking his hand through his hair, he asked impatiently, "Are you going to let me open his door?"

"No," she answered again. "I can't."

Her "I can't" was anticlimactic now. "Fine. You handle Anthony like you've handled everything else. And in case you're under the illusion that you actually *are* a Super mom, just imagine what this will be like if you take on another job."

From the look on Angela's face, he knew he'd said too much. Before he said even more, he went down the stairs.

She didn't stop him. It was a good thing he still had his jacket on because he unlocked the front door and left, not looking back.

Throughout the weekend, Angela was heartsick. She'd pushed David away one time too many. On Saturday, she felt like a zombie, working at Felice's Nieces, gift wrapping Christmas presents, acutely aware that Anthony wasn't any happier than she was.

Over and over she thought about her argument with David. She should have let him go into Anthony's room. She should have let him try.

But she'd been afraid.

Of what? That Anthony would withdraw even further than he had? How was that possible?

On Sunday—Christmas Eve—she kept her mood as light as she could, dreading the moment when Jerome would come for the kids. She was going to give her presents to them after an early supper. When they returned home from their trip with Jerome, there would be more presents that Santa brought under the tree.

"Do you think Santa will come to Dad's?" Michael asked her.

"I don't know. My guess is, he might not be sure where you'll be, so he'll leave your Christmas presents here. But you'll have your dad's presents to open."

She hoped. She hoped that was a promise Jerome made

good on. Not that he had to buy anything extravagant like a computer, but just that he remembered he was part of his kids' Christmas and giving to them was important. Especially now.

After supper, Michael and Olivia went to wait by the tree. She'd told them she'd read them "The Christmas Story" before they opened their gifts.

Anthony came up to her and, with big, brown, wide eyes asked, "Dad is going to really come and take us with him, isn't he?"

Angela felt as if her heart were cracking apart, one piece at a time. "He said he would, honey. We'll just have to see if he keeps his promise." She absolutely couldn't reassure Anthony about this, not without knowing what was in Jerome's head.

When Olivia opened her two new outfits and a Pet Doctor Barbie, she loved it all. Angela had already bought Barbie before Olivia had come home with the one Jerome had bought her. But her daughter didn't seem to mind.

Olivia concluded, "They can be sisters like you and Aunt Megan. They'll have lots of fun together."

As always, Michael was thrilled with the new truck, the sneakers he'd asked for and a stick horse he could ride around the living room.

Anthony hugged her after he opened a new game for his GameBoy and a DVD. He held on a few minutes longer than he normally would have, and she wished again that Jerome would understand the treasures he had in these kids.

After they left she would bring Santa's gifts down from her closet. She'd bought a set of CDs and books they could all listen to and little things for each of them, like coloring books, new markers, puzzles and a magnetic building set.

To her surprise, Olivia, Michael and Anthony brought her gifts, too. Each carried an envelope with "Mom" written on the front.

"What are these?" she asked.

"Christmas presents," Michael piped up, as if she should have already guessed. "David said you'd like them. He told us how to make them."

She could have cried, right there, in front of her kids. But she didn't. She smiled bravely and opened each one. Each envelope contained a drawing and another piece of paper. On that second piece of paper, each of them had written their present. She could see someone had helped Michael with his printing.

"I will dust the living room for you."

"Do you want me to do it now?" he asked eagerly. "David said anytime would be good."

She laughed. "I think dusting can wait until after you come back from your trip."

Olivia's gift was similar. "I will clean my room all by myself."

Angela gave her daughter a hug.

When Anthony handed her his present, he mumbled, "David said you'd like this." She wasn't sure when the switch had come from Coach Moore to David, but the change had been made without fuss.

"I will empty the dishwasher and put everything away."

Giving her son a hard hug, she couldn't blink away the lone tear that escaped.

To her relief, Jerome arrived on time at seven o'clock.

After he took the kids' duffels to the car, he said, "It'll take about two hours to drive where I'm going." He handed her a slip of paper. "Here's the address and phone number. They might be asleep till we get there."

"It's Christmas Eve. I doubt that. I'd like to talk to them before they go to bed."

He sighed. "This is my time with them, Angela. Tell you what. I'll give you a call when we get there so you know we arrived, and you can talk to them tomorrow."

"All right," she agreed, compromising. "But please, don't forget. Snow's supposed to fall farther north and I'll worry if you don't call."

"You'll worry if I *do* call," he jibed.

After her children left, the house was silent and Angela felt lost. She'd so wished David would call her. But he was probably with his own family, celebrating.

She brought her kids' presents downstairs from the closet in her room, and she stared at the ones she'd wrapped for David. He'd already given her kids so much. He'd given *her* so much. She missed him unbearably, knowing she'd handled everything all wrong.

After Jerome called that they'd arrived at the ski lodge, she sat alone by the tree watching the twinkling lights almost the entire night, finally going to bed around three.

It was almost 11:00 a.m. on Christmas morning when Angela's phone rang. She snatched it up, hoping it would be David, hoping it would be her kids. But it was Megan.

"Merry Christmas, sis. Where are you? You're supposed to be over here at Carly and Bo's."

Yes, she was. The open house had started with brunch at ten and was scheduled to last long into the afternoon. When Carly threw a party, she really threw a party.

Trying to inject a note of Christmas cheer into her voice, Angela said, "Merry Christmas to you, too."

"Are you coming over soon?"

"I'm just getting up. With the kids not here…" She let her voice trail off.

"What are your plans for today after Carly's party?" Megan asked.

"I don't…have plans."

"Well, you do now. Greg and I have presents for you and the kids."

"The kids won't be back until—"

"I know. But you can open yours, and we'll put theirs under the tree. This party should wind down by dinner. We'll come over then."

Angela knew she wouldn't be staying at Carly's that long. She would put in an appearance, and then come back home. Home to what, she didn't know.

David was right about this house. Why was she hanging on to it, as well as the bills that went with it? As a token of her marriage? Darn big token.

But what about the cooking show? They want to use your kitchen, a little voice who didn't want to let go asked.

They don't even know what my kitchen looks like, she answered back. Probably any kitchen would do.

After she hung up the phone, she applied makeup, put on a red, stretch-velvet tunic top and slacks. She wore her mother's pearl necklace. No amount of makeup would hide the circles under her eyes. Angela did *not* feel up to a party, but this celebration was important to Carly—a Christmas different from any she'd ever had. She was so happy with Bo and wanted to share that happiness. Angela knew if she didn't go, some of her friends might even come looking for her. Better to paste on a smile, make an appearance and then an early getaway. In her Christmasy outfit, Angela *looked* a lot cheerier than she felt.

Peering out the window at the gray sky, she saw snow beginning to fall. It had just started to lie on the pavement. After she pulled on her boots and slipped into her coat, she walked the short distance to Carly's mansion. When Carly was in college in North Carolina, she used to tour various plantations. *Gone with the Wind* was one of her favorite books. Trying to make her dreams come alive, her input had led to the plantation-style house on Danbury Way.

Carly herself opened the huge front door and gave Angela a big hug before taking her coat and handing it off to a maid. "I'm so glad you could come. I heard Jerome took the kids for the holiday. You must be missing them."

Angela's eyes filled with tears. She was. And missing David, too. Thinking fast, she replied, "That's why I'm here. To get a little Christmas cheer."

Taking her arm, Carly tugged her toward a huge tree decorated with hand-crafted ornaments.

"That's different from last year's tree," Angela couldn't help but say.

Carly laughed. "Sure is. Last year's was profession-ally decorated. This year, children from the community center made all the ornaments."

They were fashioned of construction paper and yarn, and Angela had to smile. Carly's heart was completely involved in Christmas this year.

"I did have brunch catered, though. You'll have to have some of the divine crab quiches. Bo's around here some-where. I think Megan and Greg are in the dining room."

Looking around the living room that was decorated in shades of beige and light blue, Angela saw the Vincentes, who always looked happy, and the Martins, who never looked happy. Angela hoped they didn't have another of their famous arguments here.

Just then, Bo spotted his wife, came over and put his arm around her. "Have you told her yet?" he asked Carly.

Carly's smile was absolutely radiant. Leaning close to Angela's ear, she whispered, "I'm pregnant."

Angela gave both of them huge hugs. She really was happy for them. Bo looked as happy to be a father as Carly did to be a mother.

"You're going to have to give me lots of tips on how to be a good mom," Carly suggested. "Maybe you should write a book. Molly and I would surely read it."

"You follow your instincts and your heart," Angela told Carly. "And you'll be just fine. Molly, too."

At the far end of the room, Sylvia Fulton was standing with her husband Horace. She waved to Angela and motioned to Carly.

"I'd better see what she wants," Carly said.

As his wife moved away, Bo took Angela's elbow. "Do you want me to get you something to drink? The eggnog's great."

"No, I'm fine. Really. You don't have to keep me company. I can circulate."

"Is something wrong?" he asked with concern. "You don't seem yourself."

"I'm just lonely without the kids. I'm just…" *I'm just sick that I made so many mistakes with David,* she thought but didn't say it. "I'm fine."

Zooey, who was standing with Jack, Rebecca and Joe, caught her eye.

"Thanks for asking," Angela said to Bo. "I think Zooey's trying to get my attention."

As Bo crossed to his wife, Angela moved toward Zooey and heard Rebecca say to Jack, "We're going to visit Randall later today." Randall was Jack's uncle, and Rebecca's birth father. Christmas was a time for reunions and strengthening of family bonds. At least, that's what it should be.

No sooner had Angela given Zooey a Christmas hug than the cell phone in her pocket sent out its lively tune.

"It might be the kids," she explained, feeling her heart lift as she excused herself and went down the hall to a powder room. Stepping inside, she barely noticed the marble and brass as she opened her phone. At first she thought she heard static. But then she realized what she was hearing was crying! Sobbing.

"Anthony, is that you?"

"Mom. Oh, Mommy," he sobbed.

"What's the matter, honey?" Her nine-year-old never cried if he could help it. Even with the broken arm, he'd tried to be stoic. So she was really worried. "What's wrong? Are you okay? Are your sister and brother okay?"

"No," he wailed. "Dad brought— He brought a *girl* along."

Okay, she told herself. *Stay calm. Get the facts.*

"A girl? You mean a date?" What in the blue blazes was Jerome doing with a date when he was supposed to be spending Christmas with their children?

Anthony's voice was a little steadier now. "Michael and Olivia were asleep last night when we got here. Dad put us all to bed, then I heard him talking on the phone.

After he called you, he talked to Jocelyn for a long time. I couldn't hear it all, and I thought he was just wishing her Merry Christmas."

Although Angela didn't want to put words into Anthony's mouth or thoughts into his head, she really wanted to ask, *Did she come over and stay with your dad last night?* Instead, she waited.

"So this morning we had breakfast, then he gave us a computer and he put on a CD of Christmas carols. We even sang along. But then he said he was meeting somebody to go skiing. There's a babysitter here now, and we're just supposed to watch TV!"

A babysitter, a stranger, was with her children on Christmas Day? Trying not to panic she asked, "Is this babysitter an older lady?"

She could practically hear Anthony thinking about her question. Finally he answered, "I guess she's as old as Simon's sister."

Simon's sister was sixteen. Even if Anthony was off by a couple of years, Angela didn't like the scenario at all. "What's your babysitter doing now?"

"She's reading magazines. Dad told her to call room service around four o'clock. I don't wanna eat dinner from room service, Mom. I want one of *your* dinners. I wanna be with *you*. We don't want to stay here."

The poignant note in Anthony's voice tore her heart apart. She knew if it was snowing in Rosewood, it was probably snowing harder farther north where Jerome had taken the kids to the Alpine Lodge. Her van wasn't four-wheel drive. But she wouldn't let her kids be stranded on Christmas. She wouldn't have them babysat as if they weren't important…as if they didn't matter. She could ask Megan and Greg to drive her up. Or—

"Honey, this is what I want you to do. It's going to take me a couple of hours to get there, maybe longer with the snow. If you get hungry, let the babysitter order you room service and make sure you all order whatever you want. I'll be there as soon as I can."

"If Dad comes back, should I tell him you're coming?"

"You can. It's certainly not going to be a secret when I get there."

There was a pause. Then Anthony asked, "Are you mad I called?"

"No, I'm not mad. You did the right thing. Now go out there with your sister and brother and tell them I'll be there as soon as I can to wish them a Merry Christmas in person. Anthony, you're the oldest, so you have to look after them. Okay?" She knew it was time she started giving him more responsibility in the small things so later he'd be able to accept responsibility in the larger ones. She'd wanted to keep them all babies. And they weren't. Especially Anthony.

After Anthony hung up, she clicked off her phone and took one very long, deep breath. She was going to call David. He might not even be home. He might be at his dad's. He might not want any more to do with her. But she had to show him she'd been terribly wrong by not letting him enter Anthony's room. She had to show him she wanted him in her life...*and* in her kids' lives. She had to show him how much he meant to her. She needed his advice and support.

She needed *him.*

Speed dialing his number, she hoped beyond hope he had a forgiving heart.

Chapter Thirteen

When David answered his cell phone, Angela's stomach practically turned over and her heart pounded in her ears. "David, it's Angela."

In the silence she counted the beats of her heart.

"Angela," he replied, his voice tempered. "Merry Christmas."

His greeting was definitely forced, so before he decided to hang up, she asked, "Are you in Rosewood?"

"Yes, I came home this morning."

Trudging ahead, she said softly, "I need your help."

"What's wrong?" He sounded genuinely concerned and she became more hopeful.

Quickly she told him about Anthony's call. "I have to drive up there. But it's snowing and my van's not good in snow. I wondered...I wondered if you'd drive me."

His pause was a long one. "I guess I'm the only one

you know who has four-wheel drive," he eventually responded, and she supposed she deserved that.

"No, you're not. Greg has an SUV. But, David, I was wrong the other night. Very wrong. I should have let you talk to Anthony. I'd like you to drive me, because you're involved in this, too."

"Am I?" he prodded. "What's going to happen when we get there, Angela? What if Anthony doesn't want me there any more than his father's girlfriend? Then what will you do?"

"I don't know what's going to happen. I do know Jerome's girlfriends are in and out of his life overnight. You're...different. And I think, deep down, Anthony knows that. It would help me to have you there...to have your support." She had so much more she wanted to say to David. But not like this. Not now. Not over the phone.

She held her breath, waiting for his response.

"I'll be at your place in ten minutes," he said.

"I'll be ready."

When he clicked off, Angela slipped her phone back into her pocket and went to retrieve her coat.

At home Angela thought about changing, but knew she didn't have time for that. Instead, she made a thermos of hot chocolate and grabbed a can of Christmas cookies.

By that time, David was at her front door. He looked wonderful, his blond hair catching the snow. All she wanted was to feel his arms around her, his lips on hers, his voice low and sexy in her ear.

But that might never happen again. She'd essentially pushed him out of her life, and he might never forgive her. "Thank you for doing this."

"Your kids don't deserve to be abandoned on Christmas Day." His voice was gruff and he made no move to come in.

Her wool coat was almost as warm as her ski jacket. She didn't bother with a hat as she grabbed the cookies and thermos she'd set on the foyer table, locked the door and joined David outside. When she climbed into his SUV, she saw presents on the backseat.

He noticed her looking and explained, "They're for your kids."

A lump lodged in her throat as she fastened her seat belt. The awkwardness between them was excruciating, but already the roads were getting nasty, and she didn't want to take his attention away from driving.

So…as the windshield wipers brushed snow from his line of vision, she tried casual conversation. "I thought you might be at your dad's today."

"I drove up yesterday to be with my family on Christmas Eve. My sister made dinner at the farm last night for everyone. It was nice."

She had no right to ask questions about his family, but she wanted to keep a conversation going. "Did you talk more about selling the farm?"

David gave her a sideways glance.

"Never mind. It's not any of my business. I just thought we needed something to talk about."

With obvious frustration he blew out a breath. "Yeah, I guess we do."

The windshield wipers struggled to sweep the glass clear of snow.

"Actually, I think my sister and I talked Dad out of selling the farm. At least, not the whole farm. There's been a developer who's wanted to buy it, but we discussed with Dad the possibility of just selling off *some* of the acreage. I found a man who's interested in running the dairy farm for him. He'd make an investment and share in the profits, but Dad wouldn't have to do the manual labor anymore. He could just oversee, stay living at the farmhouse, and enjoy life by not working so hard."

"Did your dad go for the idea?"

"Actually, he did."

A truck pulled out in front of them from a side road, skidded, aimed himself in the right direction again and made tracks in the snow ahead of them. David was intent on the driving.

Finally Angela couldn't stand the strain, the words inside her jumping up and down, ready to spill out. She couldn't help reaching out and touching his arm. "I know we have to talk about us. But I don't want to distract you. I just want you to know I want you in my life."

His silence was hard to take. When he spoke, he seemed to choose his words carefully. "The thing is, Angela, I won't sit on the sidelines anymore. Olivia, Michael and Anthony are your kids. But if I'm going to be an influence in their lives, you can't shut me out."

"I know," she murmured. "I realized the past few days, I don't *want* to shut you out."

Quiet for a long time, he finally asked, "Are you planning to pack up the kids and take them home?"

"I don't know. We'll just have to see what happens when we get there."

Getting there took three hours instead of two. The snow fell heavier the farther north they drove. When they reached the lodge, at least five inches of snow was mounting up on the roads.

As David took the turn into the resort, his wheels spun. But finally the powerful SUV churned up the snow and proceeded up the incline.

"They're not staying in the lodge itself," Angela explained. "They're in one of the chalets—number four."

The road was well marked and they found the chalet easily. In a matter of minutes, they were at the door, knocking.

The babysitter, a girl who was indeed around sixteen, opened the door, but Olivia, Michael and Anthony were right behind her.

"Mom!" they all yelled and began jumping up and down.

Then Anthony saw David. "Why did *he* come along?" he asked her.

"Because I asked him to come along," she answered.

"I came along for lots of reasons," David added. "Why don't we go inside and talk about them?"

The teenager looked uncomfortable. "Mr. Buffington didn't say anything about having visitors. I don't know if I should let you in."

At least the girl was responsible, Angela thought. Taking her wallet from her purse, she showed her identification. "I'm their mother. This is Mr. Moore. He's a friend of mine."

"She's our mom," Olivia said, hugging her, not caring snow was falling on her, too.

"Daddy left us here with her," Michael complained. "And there's nothing to do. The computer's still in the box, and we're tired of watching TV."

With a roll of her eyes, the teenager stepped aside, and Angela and David went in.

The chalet consisted of an efficiency kitchen and a living room with a fireplace. There was a nubby, sand-colored couch, two chairs, along with a wooden table and chairs. To the rear of the chalet were two bedrooms.

"How much do I owe you?" Angela asked the teenager, making it clear that she could leave.

"My fee goes on Mr. Buffington's account."

Taking his wallet from his jeans, David took out a bill. "But I'm sure you take tips for the holidays, right?"

The girl looked at him and smiled. "Sure do." Then she glanced at Olivia and Michael, who were happily hanging on to Angela, as well as Anthony who had gone over to sit on the couch.

Angela asked, "Do you live nearby? Will you need a ride?"

"I'm staying at the lodge with my parents. We spend Christmas here every year."

A few minutes later the babysitter zipped her jacket and was gone.

Still unsure of the situation, Angela was glad when David sat beside Anthony on the couch and explained, "I drove your mom here because the highway was snowy and she didn't think her van could handle the road conditions."

Perched on the arm of the sofa, Angela added, "More importantly, I asked David along because I knew he would understand how you felt today."

David gazed down at her son. "It must have been scary when your dad left you with someone you didn't know. Especially on Christmas."

When Anthony's eyes welled up with tears, he turned away from David.

Angela stayed perfectly still.

Putting his hand on Anthony's shoulder, David assured the nine-year-old, "It's okay to be scared, you know. It's okay to want to be with the people you love on Christmas."

"I thought Dad was going to play games with us. I thought he wanted us here."

"I know you did," David sympathized. "Maybe you need to tell him how you feel."

"He won't listen," Anthony mumbled but didn't shrug away from David's hand. "I just want to go home."

Michael piped up, "I want to see what Santa left me under our tree. Can we go home, Mom. Can we?"

Angela's gaze met David's. "For one thing, the roads are too bad to be driving now. But for another, we have some things to set straight with your dad. All of us. So we're going to stay here until he gets back."

To Michael, David said, "I know Santa probably left your presents at *your* house, but...I have a few presents in my car. Do you think you'd like to see what's under the wrappings?"

"Yes, yes, yes!" Michael said, jumping up and down as if he'd had to hold his enthusiasm in all day, and now it just had to leap out.

A few minutes later, the kids were tearing open presents. Anthony paged through his book about dinosaurs. "Wow. Look at these pictures."

Olivia's present was an art kit with markers and crayons, stickers and paper.

Michael opened a board game that they could all play. And they did. Until seven o'clock...when Jerome finally came back to the chalet with his date.

When Angela faced her ex-husband, he had the grace to look embarrassed.

After he introduced Jocelyn, who was about twenty-two, the young woman said, "Well, good." She looked at Angela. "If you're here, Jerry and I can go have dinner at the lodge."

"Over my—" Angela stopped, knowing she had to keep this polite for the kids. "I don't think that's such a great idea. The kids wanted us to take them home. Is that what you want, Jerome?"

Jerome looked from Angela to David to Olivia, Michael and Anthony. Then he sighed. "I'm going to walk Jocelyn back to her room at the lodge."

"You'll be back before midnight?" David asked, half-joking, half-serious.

"I'll be back in fifteen minutes," Jerome muttered, then left with Jocelyn.

"When he comes back, I want to talk to him alone," David said in a low voice to Angela. "Do you have a problem with that?"

"What are you going to talk about?"

"The way he made the kids feel. I think he needs to know. I also think he needs to know that he's damn lucky to have these kids. And if he doesn't pay attention to them, he's going to lose them."

"I don't mind at all if you talk to Jerome. I've never been able to get through to him. Maybe you can."

Then David finally touched her. He stroked her cheek and smiled at her. For the first time all day, she was hopeful that maybe he could forgive her. Maybe they could have a future after all.

Fifteen minutes later, when he saw Jerome tromping down the snowy walk, David went outside. Angela kept the kids busy but kept one ear attuned to raised voices or any kind of ruckus outside the door. There wasn't any.

When the two men came inside Jerome looked thoughtful. "I told David I could go bunk at the lodge with Jocelyn if you two wanted to stay here with the kids."

"Is that what you want to do?" Angela asked him.

"David explained how upset they were that I left. They might not even want me here."

"I think we should ask them," Angela decided.

Crossing over to the coffee table where the kids were still playing the board game, she asked, "How would you like it if we had one big sleepover here for Christmas?"

"You and David will stay here with us and Dad, too?" Olivia asked.

"Yes. We'll keep the fire going, tell some Christmas stories about how things were when we were kids and watch you guys fall asleep."

Anthony looked over at his dad. "Do you *wanna* stay here with us?"

There wasn't any hesitation when Jerome said, "Yes, I do. I think your mom's idea is a good one."

Michael scrambled to his feet and came over and tugged on his mother's hand. "We're hungry. Can you make us something?"

"That depends. Is there anything in the refrigerator?"

"I *did* come somewhat prepared," Jerome said, a little annoyed. "There's ham and cheese and bread, even a bag of carrots and some fruit."

"Well, there we go." Angela grinned at her kids. "I don't have to make anything. We can all make our own sandwiches. Come on, let's see who does the best job."

* * *

They'd used every pillow, blanket and spread in the chalet to make themselves comfortable in the living room. The fire was still softly flickering as Jerome snored on the sofa and Olivia, Michael and Anthony lay curled in sleeping balls in their bedrolls near the fireplace. David lay about two feet from Angela on his bedroll.

They hadn't had two minutes alone, and she knew talking would have to wait until they returned to Rosewood. She felt the pull toward him as strong as ever, but wasn't acting on it because she didn't know exactly how he felt. She didn't know exactly what would have happened if she hadn't called him today. She wanted so desperately to put everything right between them, but with three kids and an ex-husband present, that wasn't too likely to happen. She turned on her side, facing David's direction.

"Can't sleep?" his deep voice asked in the hush of night.

"I need the comfort of my old pajamas to get a really good night's sleep," she joked quietly.

Her words brought back visions of their night in New York when they hadn't been able to get enough of each other.

David turned on his side, too, and faced her. They weren't so far apart now.

The last log on the grate softly popped and sparks scattered.

"I was going to call you this afternoon," David said in a low voice.

"To wish me a Merry Christmas?" she asked lightly.

"No. To tell you I wasn't going to let you kick me out of your life."

Her gaze met his. "I thought maybe you'd given up on me."

His smile was gentle. "You're too special to give up on. I just had to get over a dented ego. *And* convince myself you needed time to understand that we had something special."

"I know we do." She reached out her hand to him.

Taking it, he gave it a squeeze and kissed her fingertips.

Any other time, any other place, his gesture would lead to lovemaking. But tonight they just held hands.

There was nothing else Angela would rather be doing.

"She wanted too much from me," Jerome said, as he and David took a walk in the snow the next morning.

"Define *too much*," David suggested reasonably.

"She wanted to jump right into having a family, and I went along with it because I didn't have a good reason not to. I mean, after all, we got married. Right? A family was next. Right? It wasn't until after Olivia was born I realized none of it was right. Not for me. Angela wanted a man who liked spending time at home. Who wanted to pitch baseballs to his kids. Who didn't feel trapped by the idea of going on a vacation with his family."

David was trying not to be judgmental. He knew that wouldn't solve anything. "Are you saying you don't want to be a father?"

Jerome's breath turned white as he blew out a long sigh. "I'm saying—the *idea* of being a father suits me better than being one. I can see you don't get that. You actually seem to like being around Anthony, Olivia and Michael. I've got to admit it's better since they're getting older. But I don't know what to do with them."

"You don't have to *do* things all the time. You can just *be* with them. Talk to them about what's important to them. Figure out what their interests are...what their talents might be."

"Did your parents teach you how to do this stuff? Mine sure didn't. My dad didn't want to be in the house any longer than he had to be. He liked cars and cards and spending time at the club."

"I was around my dad a lot," David admitted. "He taught us how to work beside him, the feeling of achievement at a job well done. And my sister and I knew our parents loved each other. That was always evident. The important thing is that your kids know you care about them. Don't promise to do something if you can't. Don't disappoint them if you can help it. If you don't know what to do with them, spend shorter amounts of time with them, but see them more often."

"If you and Angela are involved, that's what you want? Don't you want me *out* of the picture?"

"You'll never be out of the picture. You're their dad. If you're out of the picture, they're going to be hurting, and I can't make up for that."

Jerome stopped walking and faced David. "You're going to be good for her. *If* you can handle her," he warned with a wry grimace.

David laughed. That's what Jerome didn't understand. Angela didn't need to be *handled*. She needed to be loved. During their days apart, he'd realized just how much he loved her. Now he just needed the right time to tell her...the perfect time.

Later that morning Anthony came running to David as he loaded up the SUV. The nine-year-old handed him the box with the wireless keyboard. "Dad said you're going to set this up for us."

"That I am."

Looking nervous, Anthony shuffled from one foot to the other. "Mom said I should apologize to you—for throwing her phone and yelling at you the other night."

"I guess that depends on whether you feel sorry about it or not."

"I was really mad. I wanted Dad there. Instead, *you* were there."

"And it could happen again, Anthony. Because I'm going to be around."

"Because you like Mom?" His eyes were very brown, curious, looking for answers.

"Not only because I like your mom. I like you and Olivia and Michael, too." After he wedged in the boxed keyboard so it didn't slide around, he closed the back of the SUV. "Ready to start back?"

With a tentative smile, Anthony nodded.

By the time David drove back to Rosewood, the roads were plowed and salted. Aware of Angela, the way he'd been since the moment he'd met her, he wished they could carve out a few minutes alone together. He had a Christmas present for her, but he didn't want to give it to her with an audience. Every time she looked his way, he could feel her gaze on him.

The kids sang along with Christmas carols on the radio, played the alphabet game with car license plates and squabbled a bit. As they neared home, Olivia asked Angela, "When are we going to practice for Aunt Megan's wedding?"

"We're going to practice on Saturday, and we'll be all ready for New Year's Eve."

"I *love* my dress," Olivia enthused. "It's red satin and so pretty," she told David. "Maybe when you and Mom get married, I can wear a blue one."

The sudden silence in the car came from all directions.

Anthony grumbled, "Girls. All you think about is clothes."

But there was a teasing quality to his voice, rather than a protest. David wished he could see the boy's face. Glancing quickly at Angela, he saw she was staring straight ahead, not moving a muscle…maybe not even breathing.

"Your mom and I haven't talked about a wedding."

He could feel Angela's gaze on him again. When he shot her a glance, her blue eyes were big and wide and full of questions. He had questions, too. But he was hoping they could find the answers together.

A short time later he pulled into Angela's driveway. Megan's car was there, and David knew she might be inside waiting for them. Greg could be there, too. David wanted to get to know Angela's sister and her fiancé better, but he needed a few minutes with Angela before they went inside.

Making his prediction come true, Megan opened the front door. The kids climbed out and ran to her. They hugged her and chattered as she took them inside.

David went around the back of the SUV, intending to carry presents into the house. Angela joined him there. Instead of opening the back of the car, he said, "I have to tell you what's going through my head."

Angela looked worried. "If you want me to talk to Olivia and Anthony and Michael about the whole wedding thing—"

"If we talk to them, we're going to talk to them together." He encircled her with his arms and brought her close. "I want to marry you. I love you, Angela. I want us to make a home together, whether it's here…" He nodded toward the house. "Or someplace we choose together. Is that what you want?"

"Oh, David, that's *exactly* what I want. I've been doing so much thinking…and feeling. I love you. I love you in a way I've never loved anyone. Yesterday and today I realized I don't have to be in control of everything. I can lean on you, and that's okay. I just hope you have a ton of patience because I've been trying to be a Super mom for a long time, and I don't know what's going to happen with my job."

Chuckling, he tilted his forehead against hers. "We don't have to make lifelong decisions today. At least not all of them. I wanted to give you your Christmas present since we never know what's going to happen next." Taking a box from his pocket, he handed it to her. "Open it now."

It wasn't small enough for a ring box, and he knew she could see that. They'd go shopping for her engagement ring together.

Tearing off the paper and bow, she stuffed both in her pocket and lifted the lid. "Diamond and pearl earrings! David, they're beautiful. And they match my necklace exactly. I want to put them on."

"Right now?"

"Right now."

He held the box while she fastened them to her ears. "I have your presents inside. But I think you should wait and open them when the kids are in bed tonight."

"I can do that. But I don't need them. *You're* my Christmas present."

He pulled her close, his lips meeting hers. It had been a long time since they'd kissed. They were hungry for each other, yet knew they couldn't satisfy most of that hunger right here.

Still they clung, kissed, came back for more.

When David heard a noise, he broke off the kiss, wondering what it was. Then he realized Olivia, Michael and Anthony were at the living room window, peering out. They must have knocked on the glass because they were all waving. And smiling. Even Anthony.

Angela grinned at him. "I think they approve. Maybe they'll give us a few minutes alone now and then. When they go back to school after the holidays, we can spend our lunches together."

David laughed. Life with Angela was going to be an adventure…an adventure he was ready to take on.

As David danced Angela through Megan and Greg's many wedding guests, Angela loved the sense of belonging she felt being with him. As Megan's matron of honor, she'd cried with, hugged, helped dress and stood by her sister today until she'd been joined by Greg at the front of the church after a walk down the white runner. Her sister and Greg were dancing together now, swaying, gazing into each other's eyes. Megan was stunning in her ivory satin sheath. Angela had begun looking at brides' magazines herself. She and David would be shopping for engagement rings next week.

David's arm tightened around her. "I'm so glad Zooey offered to watch the kids for a few minutes so we could dance."

"It's our first dance together," Angela said breathlessly. She always felt breathless around David. Always felt excited. Special. Loved. During the past week, while the kids had been involved in activities at the community center, she and David had made love and cuddled in his big bed, talking about the future. They'd discussed selling her house, building or buying another. She'd heard yesterday that she'd won the spot on *Meals Across America,* and she was excited about embarking on a new career. David had told her he'd support whatever she wanted to do. It was an odd feeling, knowing someone was standing beside her, looking out for her, even protecting her at times. She was getting used to all of it.

The Abernathys danced by them, as did Rebecca and Joe. Rebecca just smiled knowingly and winked.

"Those neighbors of yours who you said argue all the time came tonight," David noticed.

"The Martins?" Angela knew Megan had invited all the neighbors, but she hadn't thought the Martins would accept. Their marriage was obviously on the rocks. Why would they want to attend a wedding? On the other hand, maybe that was a good reason to attend a wedding. A wedding could remind them where they'd once been, and maybe where they wanted to go.

Carly came over to David and Angela and said, "Don't worry, I don't want to cut in. I just have a question for David."

He kept his arms around her, though their feet stopped moving.

With full speed ahead, Carly went on, "I've decided to start a foundation for underprivileged youth. I know you've got your store and football and now Angela and the kids, but I really need someone with your expertise to help me. Would you consider taking a seat on the board? You not only know kids, but you have business contacts in the community, and we'll need them to set up scholarship funds. What do you think?"

When David glanced at Angela, she knew he was being considerate about her time and her plans, too.

"We'd only meet once a month," Carly interjected. "I know everybody's time is limited. Will you think about it?"

"I'll definitely think about it. A foundation for under-privileged youth could do a lot of good in Rosewood. I'd like to be part of your plans in some way."

"Great! I'll set up a meeting with some other people I have in mind within the next couple of weeks."

After Carly moved away and they resumed dancing, Angela nestled into him again.

"Anthony looks so grown-up in his tux," she mused. "I can't believe he'll be ten next month. He told me you showed him how to find sports memorabilia on the Internet. He was impressed. He asked me this morning when you were going to come live with us."

David leaned away slightly. "What did you say?"

"I told him we hadn't set the date for the wedding yet, and we wouldn't live together until after that. But I asked him how he'd feel about moving."

"Was he upset?"

"Actually, he wasn't. He suggested we all go pick out a house together. I like that idea."

"So do I," David declared, his voice husky as he leaned close to kiss her.

His tongue had just parted her lips when there was a commotion that urged them both to end the kiss. With his arm around her, he led her toward a group of people at one of the tables.

"It's Molly! Oh, my goodness. I wonder if she's gone into labor."

Her friend was doubled over, Adam at her side. "Call an ambulance," he yelled. "Now!"

Molly patted her husband's arm as she straightened. Her face was flushed, but she didn't look in dire need of the ambulance. "We have a little time," she told Adam. "Don't panic."

"Of course I'm panicking. I'm going to be a dad."

"No ambulance," she said to anyone who could hear her. "Adam's going to drive me." She looked up at him. "Unless you're in no condition to drive."

"I'll drive you." And then he swept her up into his arms, carried her through the country club ballroom and out the door.

As David watched Adam carry Molly out, he slipped his arm around Angela's waist. "Would you consider having another child? Or do you have enough with three?"

Encircling his neck with her arms she replied softly, "I'd love having a child with *you*."

David bent his head and kissed her again.

"They're gettin' mushy," Michael piped up from Angela's side.

On Angela's other side, Olivia claimed, "That's what grown-ups do when they're going to get married."

Laughing, Angela leaned away from David and saw Anthony tug on his sleeve. "Can I be your best man?"

Ruffling the nine-year-old's hair, David kept Angela close to his side. "You *and* Michael can be my best men."

Angela held out her hand to her daughter. "And you can be my maid of honor."

The five of them had formed a circle. Angela knew it was a circle that she and David would work on strengthening for the rest of their lives.

Epilogue

"Remember, whether you have an old or new kitchen, or have been living in your house ten years or thirty years, the kitchen can be the center of the family." Angela peered into the camera that came in for a close-up shot. "It's up to *you* to make it a fun and loving place to be."

Angela didn't only say those words each week, she knew they were true. The home that she, David and the kids had picked out in the older section of Rosewood had called to them from the moment they'd set foot in it, especially the country kitchen. It had been remodeled a few years ago, giving it an authentic old-fashioned look, from the blue-and-red gingham curtains on the casement window over the sink, to the small stone fireplace in the corner. It was a perfect location for taping the show.

What's more, it was perfect for their family—the Moore family.

"It's a wrap," she heard the producer of *Meals Across America* say and the bright lights suddenly dimmed.

The next moment David was beside her, bringing her into his arms. "Great show! You even make me want to eat lemon and raspberry cream pie."

She laughed. He usually stole away from his store to watch her taping. She loved the support he gave her, constantly knowing that she wasn't alone, that she had someone to depend upon if she needed him.

And she did need him…to hold her every night in their big bed and tell her that he loved her. Which he did consistently, enthusiastically and masterfully.

Laughing, she kissed him, remembering their wedding in May, their chaotic move into this house with the kids, their goodbye to Danbury Way. She'd thought she'd miss the old neighborhood, but she didn't. Not really. She was only a few blocks from it and she and her friends still met for lunch, coffee or ice cream. They talked whenever possible on the phone. Megan was also only a few streets away and they dropped in at each other's houses often.

Marion Johnson, the producer, came over to them now. "Great job, Angela, as usual. I have some good news for you. At least, I think it's good news. It should make your decision about going back to your old job easier."

Angela had taken a leave of absence from her position at Dr. Zefflinger's. The plan was when the kids went back to school in the fall, she'd go back to her office manager's position four days a week and take Fridays for the taping. She hadn't worked at Felice's Nieces since she and David had gotten married because they simply needed the time together—time together with the kids, as well as time together alone.

"What's in the works?" David asked. He'd decided to quit coaching come fall to devote more time to Carly's foundation for underprivileged youth. Carly was hiring him as its director.

"The powers that be have authorized me to ask if you'd like to do a cooking segment every day of the week. We want to extend *Meals Across America* to include several shows and we want you to have your own show. Your ratings have blown everyone away."

Angela couldn't believe what she was hearing. This was a dream come true. She could cook every day of the week and get paid for it! "What do you want the theme to be?"

Before Marion could answer, the back door opened with Michael, Olivia and Anthony tumbling in, followed close behind by Megan and Greg. The three kids had obviously just stepped out of Megan's and Greg's swimming pool with their plastered-down hair, sunburned noses and towels wrapped around their swimsuits. Megan was wearing a fuchsia sarong covered with flowers over her one-piece suit. Greg's denim shorts covered his swimsuit, though his chest was bare.

"Thank goodness you're finished taping," Megan said. "I was so afraid of barging in in the middle."

"Nope, we're finished," Angela assured them. "And if you'd barged in…well, I guess we would have just put you on TV."

"And that's *exactly* what we want," Marion told them all. "We want Angela to do what she does best—cooking for her friends and family. On some segments we'd like them to join you. What do you think, Angela?"

David filled in Megan, Greg and the kids. "They want her to have her own daily show."

Megan gave her a huge but damp hug.

Anthony was asking, "Can I really be on TV?"

David's arm went around the boy. "It could be the start of a big career for you" he joked, and Anthony grinned back, knowing he was teasing.

Angela's eyes filled with tears. She couldn't help it. Her oldest son was happier than she'd ever seen him. David made sure he spent alone time with him, doing guy things, along with including Olivia and Michael with board games and baseball games and trips to the zoo. Miraculously, Jerome was keeping to a regular visitation schedule. Though his visits were shorter, he didn't skip them now. Megan and Greg were happily married and the four of them had grown closer as couples, sometimes going out to a club together and dancing.

Angela's life couldn't be any more perfect, and she was so grateful for that.

"It's really easy for me to settle on a theme," she told Marion. "Making your kitchen your family and fun center, cooking food everyone will love to eat."

"Sounds good to me," Marion decided. "We'll run it past marketing."

Michael pulled on Angela's hand. "Can I cook, too?"

Glancing at Marion, Angela admitted, "I'm already sprouting ideas. We can have a whole week of kids' meals."

"And husbands' meals," Megan interjected, her hand in Greg's as he shook his head and groaned.

"We'll soon have the year all filled up." Marion looked ecstatic at the ideas they were throwing out.

Angela's life was definitely full…full of love for her husband…full of love for her kids…full of love for her family and friends. She wouldn't have it any other way.

After all, she could *be* the Super mom with David by her side. "What are you thinking?" her husband whispered in her ear.

"I'm thinking how very lucky I am to have met you."

With one of those smiles of his that still curled her toes, he kissed her right there in front of everybody.

And she didn't mind at all.

* * * * *

Look for the next exciting story by
Karen Rose Smith.
Falling for the Texas Tycoon
is available in February 2008!

Special
moments

We hope that the Special Edition novel you have just
finished has given you plenty of romantic
reading pleasure.

We are thrilled to have put together a section of
special free bonus features, which we hope will add to
the entertainment in each Special Edition novel.

There will be puzzles for you to do, exciting
horoscopes glimpsing what's in your future, author
information and sneak previews of books in
the pipeline!

Do let us know what you think of these
special extras by emailing
specialmoments@hmb.co.uk

For you, from us…
Relax and enjoy…

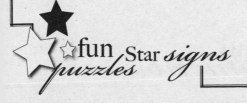

Karen Rose *Smith*

Dear Reader,

I'm a mum, so I understand my heroine's need to be the Super Mum. As a woman, I think all women are blessed with the nurturing gene. But sometimes we want to take care of everyone else and we forget to take care of ourselves!

What I love about this series is that the women on Danbury Way take care of each other. As friends, they give each other reminders and advice on everything from their love lives to taking care of kids. My heroine, Angela, finds true love and answers to the problems with her son because she realises she deserves to be happy, too – with a few gentle nudges from her sister and friends.

May we all be blessed with friends who encourage us to reach for our dreams.

All my best,

Karen Rose Smith

Special *moments*

KAREN ROSE SMITH

Award-winning author Karen Rose Smith was born in Pennsylvania. Although she was an only child, she remembers the bonds of an extended family. She and her parents lived with her grandfather and aunt until she was five, when her parents built a house next door. Since her father came from a family of ten and her mother, a family of seven, there were always aunts, uncles and cousins visiting at weekends. Family is a strong theme in her books and she suspects her childhood memories are the reason.

At college, Karen Rose began writing poetry and also met her husband-to-be. They both began married life as teachers, but when their son was born, Karen Rose decided to try her hand at a home-decorating business.

She returned to teaching for a while but changes in her life led her to writing romantic fiction. Now she writes full time. Her first romance was published in 1992; her fiftieth was released in 2005. A winner of New Jersey's Golden Leaf Award in Short Contemporary Romance, as well as the Phoenix Desert Rose Chapter's Golden Quill for Traditional Romance, she has been honoured with Cataromance.com's award for Best Special Edition of 2004. Karen Rose has also been named a finalist in the National Readers' Choice Awards, Colorado's Award of Excellence Contest, Virginia's Holt Medallion Contest and *Romantic Times* Reviewers' Choice Award. Her romances have made both the *USA TODAY* list and the Waldenbooks bestseller list for Series Romance.

Married to her college sweetheart since 1971, believing in the power of love and commitment, she envisions herself writing romance for a long time to come! Readers can e-mail Karen Rose through her website.

Kriss*kross*

Being in Love

Copyright ©2007 PuzzleJunction.com

4 letter words

Aura

Eden

Want

Warm

5 letter words

Avows

Dated

Dream

Needs

Raved

Smile

6 letter words

Admire

Enjoys

Fawned

On fire

Sacred

Tender

7 letter words

Affairs

Eyefuls

Idyllic

Salutes

Welcome

8 letter words

Caressed

Demurred

Radiates

Romantic

Special
moments

Sudoku

To solve the Sudoku puzzle, each row, column and box must contain the numbers 1 to 9.

	5							
			7	2		1		
	8		4		5		9	
								1
9	3						2	
		1	8		3	7	5	
	4		1					
				5	9		6	
		5			6			

Horoscopes

Dadhichi is a renowned astrologer and is frequently seen on TV and in the media. He has the unique ability to draw from complex astrological theory to provide clear, easily understandable advice and insights for people who want to know what their future may hold.

In the twenty-five years that Dadhichi has been practising astrology, face reading and other esoteric studies, he has conducted over 8,500 consultations. His clients include celebrities, political and diplomatic figures and media and corporate identities from all over the world.

Aries
21 March - 20 April

A stroke of good fortune is likely this month as the Sun and Jupiter occupy one of the luckiest sectors of your horoscope. You'll feel healthy and in the mood to get out and about, especially after the 8th. Romance is favoured due to Venus in your marital sector. After the 18th put aside some time for a special love affair.

Taurus
21 April - 21 May

Children can be a problem for you this month as you try to figure out their strategies. Between the 2nd and the 10th you should call a spade a spade or risk having to do double takes on serious issues. A sudden spending spree on the 15th may later cause regret.

Special moments

Gemini
22 May - 22 June

Squabbles over money aren't worth it, especially with Christmas around the corner. Think twice before pointing the finger and try to be conciliatory in your discussions. Home affairs feature strongly, particularly between the 2nd and the 4th. On the 19th a work-related matter is clarified for you.

Cancer
23 June - 23 July

You're holding on to a lot of negative feelings and they have to be released, especially around the 10th. By speaking your mind you'll clear the air and set the trend for a much more comfortable and enjoyable Christmas. Confusion over banking or other finances around the 14th is purely your own doing.

Leo
24 July - 23 August

Neighbours come into clearer focus as you develop stronger ties with them. Around the 5th a relative or sibling is back on the scene and gives you a chance to reconnect and share memories. Health matters are a concern but aren't serious. Don't make them any worse than they are.

Virgo
24 August - 22 September

An unexpected lift in income is likely, particularly in the second week of the month. This will give you the chance to beautify your home and living space. You have a taste for some expensive items like cars, boats and electronic devices. It is Christmas after all, so why not enjoy splurging a little on yourself?

Libra
23 September - 23 October

You are thoroughly eye-catching this month and your passionate aura will attract many new acquaintances. By the 20th a new friendship will blossom into a fully-fledged relationship, if you want. Be careful that divided loyalties don't ruin the experience. Don't keep secrets.

Scorpio
24 October - 22 November

Distance romance continues to fascinate you and even if you haven't met an internet buddy you'll be dreaming about them and unable to concentrate on anything else. Between the 10th and 12th take a trip and finally connect with the person of your dreams. Don't let your rose-coloured glasses detract from the truth.

Sagittarius
23 November - 21 December

Your self-confidence is at an all-time high and between the 2nd and 15th your popularity will increase to peak levels. Expect your generous nature to be impinged upon around the 17th. Balance give and take to make this Christmas a perfect one for all concerned.

Special
moments

Capricorn

22 December - 20 January

Staying low key is the secret to success this month. Between the 8th and 12th you'll prefer your own company and will discover and remedy some things about yourself which have been bothering you. Once this meditative phase is over you'll be ready to start a new and positive chapter in your life.

Aquarius

21 January - 18 February

The meaning of life and death will occupy your mind but don't make that a habit in the days leading up to Christmas. There'll be plenty of time to contemplate the Universe after the fun times. The health of an older member of the family will worry you around the 12th. Giving generously will give you an unusual sense of satisfaction.

Pisces

19 February - 20 March

A passionate affair is likely to backfire, especially if you haven't taken the time to study someone's character. You will be confused, relying on other people's opinions to dictate the course of this friendship. Use your intuition to make up your mind. Things become clearer with a sudden intuition around the 28th.

© Dadhichi Toth 2007
For more you can visit Dadhichi
at www.astrology.com.au

Poet's Corner

```
E  M  M  R  K  M  M  M  K  L  N  R  K
R  L  P  N  N  R  E  O  C  D  O  T  R
X  L  E  W  M  P  H  S  R  H  X  R  H
P  I  A  G  I  Y  O  Y  P  C  M  R  M
A  T  Z  C  Y  N  H  A  M  Z  E  W  V
L  E  N  K  N  G  T  B  N  E  T  A  B
I  R  A  E  E  E  R  D  B  L  R  N  U
N  A  T  B  M  T  K  A  D  X  E  L  H
O  T  S  T  O  M  R  L  N  M  F  C  L
D  U  F  T  T  D  A  L  K  N  I  K  M
E  R  Z  L  I  R  R  A  K  T  M  C  L
M  E  W  R  O  G  Z  B  S  N  L  I  Y
O  D  E  H  N  I  A  R  F  E  R  R  R
C  X  C  S  C  O  U  P  L  E  T  E  I
P  K  F  R  R  L  N  B  N  P  M  M  C
N  O  I  S  S  E  R  P  X  E  X  I  L
H  E  R  O  I  C  V  D  L  H  P  L  L
```

©2007 PuzzleJunction.com

BALLAD	HEROIC	ODE
BARD	HYMN	PALINODE
CHORAL	LIMERICK	REFRAIN
COUPLET	LITERATURE	RHYME
ELEGY	LYRIC	SONNET
EMOTION	METAPHOR	STANZA
EPIC	METRE	STICH
EXPRESSION	MORCEAU	VERSE

Special *moments*

Connect-it

Playthings
Copyright ©2007 PuzzleJunction.com

Each line in the puzzle below has three clues and three
answers. The last letter in the first answer on each line is the
first letter of the second answer, and so on. The connecting
letter is outlined, giving you the correct number of letters for
each answer (the answers in line 1 are 4, 6 and 6 letters).
The clues are numbered 1 to 8, with each number containing
3 clues for the 3 answers on the line. But here's the catch!
The clues are not in order - so the first clue in the line is not
necessarily for the first answer. Good luck!

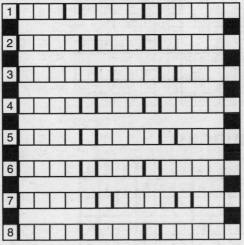

Clues:

1. Spinning toys. Possibility. Radio noise.
2. Hovel. Girls' toys. Dog enclosure.
3. Flying toys. Muffler. Reduce in size.
4. Boys' toys. Banquet. Moorage.
5. Book of maps. Slow dance. Playground toy.
6. Glove toy. Sag. Large leaf.
7. Bee house. Asian temple. Toy on a string.
8. Stuffed toy. Beast of burden. Give in.

KRISSKROSS

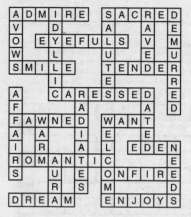

SUDOKU

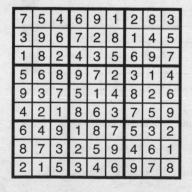

WORDSEARCH

```
E M M R K M M M K L N R K
R L P N N R E O C D O T R
X L E W M P H S R H X R H
P I A G I Y O Y P C M R M
A T Z C Y N H A M Z E W V
L E N K N G T B N E T A B
I R A E E R D B L R N U
N A T B M T K A D X E L H
O T S T O M R L N M F C L
D U F T T D A L K N I K M
E R Z L I R R A K T M C L
M E W R O G Z B S N L I Y
O D E H N I A R F E R R R
C X C S C O U P L E T E I
P K F R R L N B N P M M C
N O I S S E R P X E X I L
H E R O I C V D L H P L L
```

CONNECT-IT

1	T	O	P	S	T	A	T	I	C	H	A	N	C	E
2	D	O	L	L	S	H	A	C	K	E	N	N	E	L
3	S	H	R	I	N	K	I	T	E	S	C	A	R	F
4	W	H	A	R	F	E	A	S	T	R	A	I	N	S
5	A	T	L	A	S	E	E	S	A	W	A	L	T	Z
6	F	R	O	N	D	R	O	O	P	U	P	P	E	T
7	P	A	G	O	D	A	P	I	A	R	Y	O	Y	O
8	T	E	D	D	Y	I	E	L	D	O	N	K	E	Y

Enjoy this sneak preview of

The Couple Most Likely To
by Lilian Darcy

Available in January 2008

The Couple Most Likely To

by

Lilian Darcy

"I pushed you away because I felt so damn guilty, Stacey."

Jake heard the words that came out of his mouth after the long silence and didn't know if he could follow through with the full truth, even now. Was this what he'd meant by talking? Had he intended to make this much of a confession?

He'd driven here without rehearsing his lines, without much rational thought at all. He'd just known he needed to see her again tonight, not wait for some awkward moment when they ran into each other at the hospital.

As soon as he'd entered her house he'd felt the old attraction flare once again. He'd barely taken in the decor, just a vague impression of warmth and color and quirkiness, the kind of detail you promised yourself you'd take a closer look at next time.

And then the first thing he'd done was apologize, because there was so much he regretted when it came to Stacey and their shared past. But could he talk about it?

"Guilty?" she echoed. "Because Anna came too soon? How was that your fault? The doctors told us—"

"Because it let me off the hook. It opened the door to the original plan, the one we'd had to let go of when we found out you were pregnant. You know the saying. Be careful what you wish for."

Tears filled her eyes. "You *wished* for—"

He swore harshly. "No! Of course I didn't wish for us to lose Anna! But I would never have chosen at that age to get married and be a father and settle down in Portland, Stacey. I wanted you, but I didn't want the whole traditional package. Not then. Not at eighteen."

"And now?"

"We're not talking about now. But, no, I don't see myself ever going that route, I have to say."

"Because it's boring? Narrow?"

"Because it's…"

Too scary, and too hard.

Anna had taught him this. Most men—boys—have pretty simplistic attitudes to life at eighteen. Love is love. Grief is grief. Freedom is freedom. You want what you want. No ambivalence. No excuses. Until Stacey's pregnancy he'd never imagined you could tear yourself in two with such conflicting, opposing emotions— emotions that simply had no way to coexist. Loving Stacey became a burden. Loving Anna was a burden, also, and every bit as heavy.

"Because it's just not for me," he finished after a moment. "It's still not. And it definitely wasn't for me back then. There were times—a lot of times—when

I just wanted the whole situation to go away. Like for some superhero to fly up into space—" he mocked himself with words and tone "—and reverse the rotation of the earth so that time would spin itself back to the moment before I *didn't* pick up a pack of condoms the night of the prom, or something. It wasn't logical. It was never logical or rational or thought out, Stacey. I just wanted the situation to go away," he repeated.

"And then it did."

"And then it did."

"And I was racked with grief, while you—"

"I was, too. Never doubt that! Only I didn't have the right to be, I only had the right to feel guilty, because at some level I'd made it happen. Again, not rational. We were both in a mess. For a while, I tried to pick up the idea of us traveling, going to college together somewhere different. Like New York."

"I remember you talked about New York."

"You weren't interested. You didn't want to know. You wanted me to stay at Portland State."

"I needed *time,* for heaven's sake!"

"I know," he answered quietly. "I just couldn't see it then. Of course you did. But even if I'd given it to you, I'm not sure that it would have helped, because I wasn't ever going to let myself be happy with you after we lost Anna."

"Because you didn't think you deserved to get what you'd always wanted—the two of us *and* the wide horizons."

"That's right."

"Oh, Jake…" She didn't sound angry anymore.

"I picked the fights. I did push you away. I'm so sorry about that, Stacey, believe me. When you told me we were finished, it hurt like hell, but I felt like it had to happen. It was inevitable. There was a relief, too. Cosmic justice had been served."

"Jake…"

"I was eighteen. *We* were eighteen." To both of them, it sounded so impossibly young.

He put his arm around her and she leaned in, not away. Her head dropped to his shoulder. They stared at the flames. He felt a cloak of peace settle over his shoulders. Peace and trust.

"Tonight, when I said her name…" Jake revealed. "You're the only one I can say her name to, Stacey. My mom and dad, maybe, but it's still not the same."

"No. It wouldn't be."

Her bare arm felt warm beneath his hand. Her hip bumped his and he realized their thighs were pressing together, separated only by the fabric of his jeans and her frothy skirt. None of this was about sex, though, it was about shared pain and mutual support.

"I said something about her to my mother, once," she said quietly, after a minute. "Maybe five years ago? I used her name. *After Anna died.* Do you know what Mom said?"

"Tell me."

"'*Who's Anna?*' Mom had forgotten that we ever named her."

"She'd forgotten? The name of her own lost grand-daughter?"

"I know. It felt like a punch in the gut."

He turned her into his arms and said against the softness of her hair, "You are a miracle, Stacey."

"Because I'm not like my mother?" she whispered.

"Yes!"

He couldn't speak.

He had more to remember.

Those awful moments when they'd had to break the news to their respective parents that Stacey was pregnant. They'd announced their plan to marry at the same time. He knew his parents had had doubts and concerns, but they'd expressed them in the context of their love and support, and they'd swallowed a lot of their fears, ready to just be there, rather than preach.

Stacey's mother had been far more vocal, all of it a variation on the theme of, "How could you do this to me?" How could Stacey and Jake embarrass Trisha Handley with a teen pregnancy in front of her friends? How could they make her a grandmother, when she was only forty-three? And if they thought they'd be able to dump the baby on her for free child care whenever they felt like it, it wasn't going to happen, because Bob Handley's company was transferring him to San Diego in the spring, thanks very much, so she wouldn't be around.

He wasn't surprised that Stacey had chosen to stay in Portland when her parents and her younger sister had moved. She'd toughed out her freshman year at Portland State, earning a couple of incompletes when they lost the baby, and she'd stayed on there after Jake himself had left town. She'd moved into one of the college dorms when her parents sold their house, continued her degree part-time while she worked, and, he suspected, had remained independent of her family ever since.

He might question her choices and her priorities, but he would never question her courage.

He held her closer, feeling the heat from the gas fire against his legs. She made no move to push him away, and time seemed to slow while the universe shrank to this one point of sanity and rightness. He and Stacey, holding each other, seventeen years too late. He pressed his cheek against hers, needing the touch of her skin. She rubbed her face against his jaw like a cat, and he could smell the soft, flowery fragrance she must have dabbed below her ears at the beginning of the evening.

"Oh, Jake…"

He didn't intend to kiss her. He really didn't. But she pressed her lips to his cheek…it wasn't an intentionally sexual or inviting gesture, and yet it had the same effect. This close, he wanted her, and his body reacted to the signals she sent, even if she didn't know she was sending them.

"Stace…" He turned his head the necessary inch and found her mouth, sweet and soft, while it was still imprinting those chaste, emotional kisses on his skin—the kind of kisses she might have given a crying child. "Stace…"

The kiss changed.

She made a small sound of protest in her throat.

Protest or need, he couldn't tell.

Mixed signals.

He interpreted them the way he wanted, supported by the evidence of her arms holding him tighter, her body going pliant and soft, her lips parting to welcome him in. Their tongues met and swirled together, and he remembered. They used to kiss for hours, long ago. They burned each other up.

Tonight, she tasted of chocolate and wine and her hair smelled like strawberries. He felt the push of her breasts and the bump of her hips. He slid his hands over the back of her skirt, loving the taut curves he could feel beneath the swishy fabric.

Her fingers stroked his neck, ran up into his hair. His mouth wasn't enough for her and she kissed his whole face—his closed lids, his cheekbones, his forehead and back to his eager lips—as if she had to learn every contour by heart while she could.

MILLS & BOON
Special Edition

On sale 21st December 2007

The Marrying Kind
by Judy Christenberry

John was a millionaire, a player, a catch. But he'd never be a husband. Diane might be the quintessential forever kind of woman, but he was confident he could avoid that trap. That is, until he kissed her.

The Couple Most Likely To
by Lilian Darcy

Stacey was shocked when Jake Logan was hired by her hospital – the hotshot was her school sweetheart! Times have changed since they last saw each other – it's not young love, but it could be something deeper.

Hometown Cinderella
by Victoria Pade

Eden Perry had always been the ugly duckling. But her gorgeous transformation stunned Cameron Pratt. Could the way she looked on the outside conquer the fears of the vulnerable woman inside?

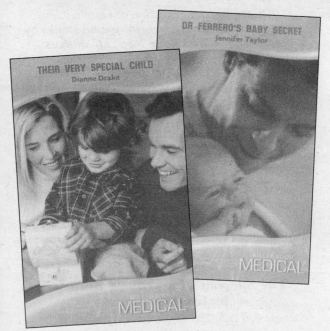

MILLS & BOON®
MEDICAL™
Proudly presents

Brides of Penhally Bay

A pulse-raising collection of emotional,
tempting romances and heart-warming stories by
bestselling Mills & Boon Medical™ authors.

January 2008
The Italian's New-Year Marriage Wish
by Sarah Morgan

Enjoy some much-needed winter warmth with
gorgeous Italian doctor Marcus Avanti.

February 2008
The Doctor's Bride By Sunrise
by Josie Metcalfe

Then join Adam and Maggie on a 24-hour rescue mission
where romance begins to blossom as the sun starts to set.

March 2008
The Surgeon's Fatherhood Surprise
by Jennifer Taylor

Single dad Jack Tremayne finds a mother for his
little boy — and a bride for himself.

*Let us whisk you away to an idyllic Cornish town —
a place where hearts are made whole*

COLLECT ALL 12 BOOKS!

MILLS & BOON®

MEDICAL™

proudly presents

Brides of Penhally Bay

Featuring Dr Nick Tremayne

*A pulse-raising collection of emotional, tempting romances and
heart-warming stories — devoted doctors, single fathers,
Mediterranean heroes, a Sheikh and his guarded heart,
royal scandals and miracle babies…*

Book Two

THE ITALIAN'S NEW YEAR MARRIAGE WISH

by Sarah Morgan

On sale 5th January 2008

A COLLECTION TO TREASURE FOREVER!
One book available every month

4 Books
and a surprise gift!

We would like to take this opportunity to thank you for reading this Mills & Boon® book by offering you the chance to take FOUR more specially selected titles from the Special Edition series absolutely FREE! We're also making this offer to introduce you to the benefits of the Mills & Boon® Reader Service™—

- ★ **FREE home delivery**
- ★ **FREE gifts and competitions**
- ★ **FREE monthly Newsletter**
- ★ **Exclusive Reader Service offers**
- ★ **Books available before they're in the shops**

Accepting these FREE books and gift places you under no obligation to buy, you may cancel at any time, even after receiving your free shipment. Simply complete your details below and return the entire page to the address below. You don't even need a stamp!

YES! Please send me 4 free Special Edition books and a surprise gift. I understand that unless you hear from me, I will receive 6 superb new titles every month for just £3.10 each, postage and packing free. I am under no obligation to purchase any books and may cancel my subscription at any time. The free books and gift will be mine to keep in any case.

E7ZEF

Ms/Mrs/Miss/Mr ....Initials ....
BLOCK CAPITALS PLEASE
Surname ....
Address...

....

....Postcode ....

Send this whole page to:
UK: FREEPOST CN81, Croydon, CR9 3WZ